THE TERROR OF TRANSMOGRIFICATION!

"We can't have a fly in here!" [illegible]ward the Slime Monster yelled in real panic [illegible] could intermingle with ours, causing [illegible] damage!"

There was somethin[illegible] the fly. Something that was [illegible]

"Toads?" De[illegible]d toads—"

But there w[illegible]pping. Edward stared at th[illegible]g things, in what might have [illegible]r.

"Bunnies? [illegible] his voice barely a whisper. . . .

DON'T MISS THESE OTHER HILARIOUS SERIES BY CRAIG SHAW GARDNER . . . *THE EBENEZUM TRILOGY* AND *THE BALLAD OF WUNTVOR*

"A lot of fun! I could hardly wait to find out what was going to happen next!"

—Christopher Stasheff, author of *The Warlock Rock*

"A delight for all fans of funny fantasy!"

—Will Shetterly, author of *Cats Have No Lords*

"A slapstick romp worthy of Laurel & Hardy . . . but I warn you not to read it late at night—the neighbors will call the cops when you laugh down the walls!"

—Marvin Kaye, author of *The Incredible Umbrella*

"A bizarre, witty, delightful fairy tale for grown-ups!"

—Mike Resnick, author of *Stalking the Unicorn*

Ace Books by Craig Shaw Gardner

The Ebenezum Trilogy

A MALADY OF MAGICKS
A MULTITUDE OF MONSTERS
A NIGHT IN THE NETHERHELLS

The Ballad of Wuntvor

A DIFFICULTY WITH DWARVES
AN EXCESS OF ENCHANTMENTS
A DISAGREEMENT WITH DEATH

The Cineverse Cycle

SLAVES OF THE VOLCANO GOD
BRIDE OF THE SLIME MONSTER
REVENGE OF THE FLUFFY BUNNIES

REVENGE OF THE FLUFFY BUNNIES

CRAIG SHAW GARDNER

ACE BOOKS, NEW YORK

This book is an Ace original edition,
and has never been previously published.

REVENGE OF THE FLUFFY BUNNIES

An Ace Book / published by arrangement with
the author

PRINTING HISTORY
Ace edition / October 1990

ISBN: 0-441-71833-7

Ace Books are published by The Berkley Publishing Group,
200 Madison Avenue, New York, New York 10016.
The name "ACE" and the "A" logo
are trademarks belonging to Charter Communications, Inc.

PRINTED IN THE UNITED STATES OF AMERICA

10 9 8 7 6 5 4 3 2 1

ACKNOWLEDGMENTS

Yes, and as yet another trilogy bites the dust, it's time to place the thanks and/or blame. From my misspent youth, I have to thank Channels 8, 10, and 13 in Rochester, New York, for *Swashbuckler*, *Chiller*, and *Son of Hercules Theatres*—fine programming for a growing boy. From my misspent adulthood, I should thank the fine folks at the Orson Welles, Brattle, Coolidge Corner, Park Square, and Kenmore Square Theatres, as well as all the other wonderful repertory houses that have come and (mostly) gone in the Boston area in the last twenty years. These places made it possible for me to see a pair of Toshiro Mifune samurai films in the afternoon, a Marlene Dietrich double bill in the evening, followed by *The Night of the Living Dead* at midnight. Wow! What a great way to waste your life. Thanks also go to all those folks who also made the B-films, especially Samuel Fuller, Ray Harryhausen, George Pal, Gene Autry, Dorothy Lamour, and Johnny Weismuller, who inspired some of the worlds herein.

It's also time to once again thank all the usual suspects who helped to make this series what it is today: Elisabeth, for efforts beyond the call of duty; Jeff, Victoria, Richard, Mary, Charlotte, and Maggie for their cogent criticism; Tamara, who did the impossible and kept me organized; Merrilee and all the helpful folks at Writers House, who keep me in business; and the ever-cooperative crew at Ace (Hi Susan! Hi Beth! Hi John!), and, of course, the person to whom this book is dedicated:

GINJER

A wonderful editor and a good friend.

1

She felt so peculiar.

"Ah hahahaha!" the man in her life laughed heartily. "Ah hahahaha!"

Mrs. Roger Gordon, Sr. found that she wanted to laugh as well. She wanted to toss back her head and let the mirth bubble up from her belly. She wanted to hang onto this dear, silver-suited man by her side until the laughter consumed her. But she restrained herself. After all, she was a woman of mature years, not some giddy schoolgirl.

Still, she did feel like a *changed* woman of mature years. She found she no longer had any interest in the bridge club, or the Japanese beetles in the back garden, or the fact that her son, Roger Jr. , never bothered to call her.

Instead, she had this overwhelming urge to destroy.

"Hee," she remarked, quite unintentionally.

"Oh, Mrs. G.!" her suitor enthused. "It will be so wonderful, gaining absolute mastery of the Cineverse with you by my side!"

"Why, Mr. M.!" she answered coquettishly, even though she really had no idea what he was talking about. Still, his enthusiasm was so infectious!

"Hee hee," she added.

Perhaps she was being too hard on herself. A widow in her situation tended to get a bit set in her ways—she had seen it happen to her friends, and she wanted to guard against that sort of thing happening to her. Besides, she reminded herself, she wasn't that old. She had plenty of good years left, years that could be very well spent with the right sort of man.

The right sort of man squeezed her elbow affectionately.

Mr. M., as she liked to call him, even though her son had informed her that his real name was Menge the Merciless. Not your usual name, but she thought it had a certain charm. He smiled at her, displaying his single shining gold-capped tooth among the pearly white molars. A man of his age, and he still had his own teeth. That certainly said something about his character. Besides, she always was a sucker for a pencil-thin mustache.

He leaned close to her.

"Ah hahahaha!" he whispered in her ear.

The way that man laughed sent a chill down her spine.

"Hee hee hee," she replied demurely.

She was certainly glad that Mr. M.—Menge, she reminded herself—was here to help her get acclimated. Heaven knew, these surroundings would take some getting used to. She was still a bit disoriented by how fast things had been happening around her. One minute, she had been at home, looking through her keepsake drawer, and had stumbled on this cheap plastic ring, one of those prizes her son always used to save from cereal boxes. The next thing she knew, she was surrounded by thick blue smoke. And when that smoke disappeared an instant later, Mrs. Gordon discovered she was no longer standing in her bedroom, but had somehow been transported to a sunny beach, surrounded by teenagers with surfboards. And her son, Roger—who was far too old for that sort of thing—had been there, too.

Well, what was she to think? She demanded an explanation, but Roger, as usual, seemed completely incapable of giving her one. She sometimes wondered what kind of job her son could do in public relations if he couldn't even communicate with his own mother.

Fortunately for her, that was when her dear Menge had arrived—also, oddly enough, in a cloud of blue smoke. And he had, of course, been much more willing than her own son to explain everything to her, including the workings of that large machine, the Zeta Ray, which he had brought along with him.

She still wasn't too certain of the exact meaning of the

events that immediately followed. First, Menge had explained that he, regretfully, had brought his machine to fry her son's brain. She had objected—it was a mother's duty, after all—until Mr. M. had explained that exposure to the ray would actually make Roger much more polite. Even a mother couldn't argue with results like that.

Some of the other people on the beach, however, still felt the need to argue, and more than argue. Roger wasn't too keen on getting his brain fried, and his friends did a lot of shouting and carrying on.

And then there was this jungle person there—Splabana, Zabana, something like that—who had physically attacked dear Menge. The machine had gone off as the two men struggled, the ray shooting out to bathe her in its golden light.

After that, everything had been different.

Not that she had had much of a chance to think about it. Menge had swept her away almost immediately in another burst of blue smoke.

And they had arrived here, a place that seemed to be the very opposite of the sunny beach. The sky was heavily overcast, the ground covered by a layer of fog, and before them was a great building, as colorless as the rest of their surroundings. Mrs. Gordon found something about the building disturbingly familiar, even though she couldn't quite place the architecture. Perhaps the huge structure was some sort of fortress, maybe even a medieval castle. It looked like some odd combination of the two, but there was something more to the place, something unpleasant. If, she reflected, you added a bit of the sort of municipal structure where you had to stand in line for hours to get your registration renewed—yes, that was the building exactly!

Her feeling of unnameable dread identified, Mrs. Gordon somehow felt oddly at peace with her surroundings. So what if everything here only showed variations on shades of gray? Menge's silver suit no longer shone. Even the flowered print of her dress seemed dulled, as if this place wanted to drain the color away. But all this didn't upset her in the least.

Now, for some reason, the dreariness seemed to cheer her up.

"Hee," she remarked. "Hee hee hee."

"Mrs. G.," Menge announced with a flourish of his cape. "I would like to welcome you to our secret headquarters."

Secret headquarters? That certainly sounded mysterious—and important! And Menge was going to share it specially with her? As mature a woman as she was, Mrs. Gordon was beginning to feel more like that giddy schoolgirl with every passing minute.

"I am quite overwhelmed, Mr. M."

The man in her life took both her shoulders in his strong hands, and gently turned her to face him. His pencil-thin mustache quivered ever so slightly as he looked into her eyes.

"Mrs. G.," Menge purred. "We have known each other for some time, but I have never asked you a very important question."

She stared back at him. Her heart thumped heavily in her chest. What could this mean?

He took her right hand in his.

"What is your first name?"

"Why, Mr. M.!" She found herself blushing. In the oddest sense, the question seemed very personal. She hardly ever used her first name—except with her very closest friends.

"Antoinette," she replied softly.

"Antoinette?" Mr. M. echoed. "It is a lovely name."

She found herself blushing all over again. But she could not let this deeply personal moment fade away. She and this handsome, bald man in the silver suit were closer than they had ever been before, but she felt they could be closer still.

She looked deep into Menge's small but sensitive eyes.

"Now that you know my first name," she began, a slight catch in her voice, "I should ask the same of you."

"Indeed you could," he replied sympathetically, "but I would not answer you. There are certain things better left buried.'' He paused for a moment, then added quickly: ''You may call me Mengy, if you wish.''

''Mengy?'' she asked.

He smiled as she said it. ''It's a name they called me on the surfing world. Frankly, it annoyed me when others used it. But, coming from your lips, the name becomes a song to my ears.''

''Mengy,'' she repeated in a hoarse half-whisper.

''Antoinette,'' he answered firmly as he pulled her close. ''Ah hahahaha.''

He looked down at her, then leaned his head forward, his lips almost touching her upturned face. His pencil-thin mustache tickled her nose. She closed her eyes in anticipation as she leaned forward as well.

''Is this how you''—a new voice interrupted—''obey my orders?''

Mengy snapped to attention. Mrs. Gordon opened her eyes as she turned to face the newcomer, her lips still longing for that kiss that had been only an instant away.

A man in a green snakeskin smoking jacket stared haughtily at them both.

''Doctor Dread!'' Menge announced. ''I was merely showing the fortress to our newest recruit.''

''Newest recruit?'' Dread asked incredulously. ''And who gave you''—he paused ominously—''permission to bring in new recruits? Especially''—he paused again, his eyes darting critically from Antoinette to Menge and back again—''*this* kind of recruit!''

Mrs. Gordon wasn't sure she liked this fellow, even if he was a doctor. This Dread person was thinner than Menge—too thin, really. Dread also sported a pencil-thin mustache. Still, Mrs G. thought, such a mustache did not suit the doctor's pinched face anywhere near as well as it did Menge's more robust, manly looks. And there was something about the way Dread spoke that she found irritating—maybe it was the way he paused all the time. Whatever it was, it didn't add up to a very favorable first impression. In all fairness, she didn't think this so-called doctor was good enough to shine Mengy's silver shoes.

"No, no, Doctor Dread," Menge added quickly. Did he have to be so obsequious? This was a side of her man that she had never seen before.

"You don't understand certain important things about our new recruit," Menge continued, "such as the fact that she has relatives in very high places."

"Relatives?" Dread snapped, as if just the mention of that word was enough to drive him to fury. "Ever since Big Bertha convinced me to employ her good-for-nothing brother Louie, I have had enough of"—he paused in order to summon enough venom for the final word—"*relatives*!"

"But you haven't heard me out!" Menge insisted. Mrs. G. was glad he was getting a bit more forceful. This was the Mr. M. she found so attractive, the man equally adept at building a rec room on Earth or controlling the Zeta Ray in the Cineverse.

Menge put his arm around her.

"This woman is the mother of Roger Gordon."

Dread's mouth opened, his fury forgotten. "Mother?" He paused, so astonished that he forgot to be sinister. "Roger—Gordon?"

With the mention of her son's name, Antoinette found her anger inexplicably on the rise, as if Dread's fury had been contagious.

"He's not much of a son!" she spat. "I can't even remember the last time he called!"

"I think it only fair to mention," Menge continued smoothly, "that our new recruit has also been zapped by the Zeta Ray!"

"The Zeta Ray?" Dread's pinched face broke into a childlike grin, as if he had suddenly discovered today was Christmas. "Mother? Roger Gordon? Zeta Ray?" He began to laugh anemically. "Heh. Hehheh. Heh heh heh."

"Ah hahahaha!" Menge answered. "Ah hahahaha!"

The levity was contagious. Antoinette couldn't help but join in. "Hee hee hee hee! Hee hee hee hee!"

"Menge!" Dread exclaimed. "You are to be—congratulated. With Roger Gordon's mother at our side, no one will be able to stop the—Change! Heh! Hehhehheh!"

They all laughed some more.

Dread cut the laughter abruptly with a wave of his snakeskin glove.

"Enough frivolity! We need to make"—he hesitated suggestively—"arrangements for the final stages of the—Change! Meet me in the—throne room in five minutes. And bring your"—this time, he paused too suggestively for Antoinette's liking—"new recruit!"

Dread turned with a flurry of his snakeskin cape. He rapidly climbed the slate staircase leading to the gray edifice before them, disappearing a moment later through one of a pair of twenty-foot-tall, dull steel doors.

There was a moment of uncomfortable silence between the two who remained outside.

"We really know so little about each other," Antoinette sighed at last. "Why, until now, I didn't even know you were in someone else's employ."

"In someone else's employ?" Her man shook his head firmly. "Not for long, Mrs. G. Not for long." He once again placed his hands upon her shoulders. "Meeting you on Earth, helping to build your rec room, the so-called accident with the Zeta Ray—I realize now that none of these things were mere chance! No, Antoinette Gordon and Menge the Merciless are two names that together speak of destiny!"

He squeezed her shoulders. She had never seen him look so intense!

"Even Doctor Dread is as nothing before us!" He let go of her to ball both his hands into fists. "Soon, Menge the Merciless will control the Cineverse, with the lovely Antoinette by his side!"

He stopped to look up the stairs, his grin of triumph replaced by an uncertain frown.

"But come!" he said as he took her hand. "We cannot be late for the throne room. Everything must seem normal until we can make our move. Then, after careful planning—

ultimate triumph! Ah hahahaha! Ah hahahaha!"

Antoinette smiled as the Merciless One led her up the stairs. She did like a man who knew his own mind! With him by her side, she didn't even care about Earth or her past life. With Menge, her life was all brand new.

She had the feeling that all sorts of interesting things were going to happen!

2

All was darkness—a hot, damp darkness, as if the heat of noon had forgotten to go away. Delores couldn't see a thing.

Something roared loudly, out there in the still air of the endless night.

Something else screamed.

"Sorry," the voice of Edward the Slime Monster whispered in her ear.

"Sorry?" Delores replied, surprised at the venom in her own voice. "Here I am, one minute, standing on a sunny beach, directly across from the man I love, and the next, I am whisked away by a creature made of putrescent muck to a place that would make the Black Hole of Calcutta look like a vacation resort, and all you can say is—you're sorry?"

"Um," Edward replied, "how about if I say I'm *very* sorry?"

"Nope," Delores replied firmly. "It doesn't wash."

"Slime monsters never do," Edward admitted. "If you get us too near water, it can become very messy."

"Look," Delores interjected as reasonably as she could. "If you're *really* sorry, why don't you take me back to the beach?"

Delores felt droplets of slime hit her exposed neck and arm.

"I can't," the Slime Monster admitted with a quaver in his voice. Could that be a quaver of fear? What, Delores thought with a shiver of her own, could a slime monster be afraid of?

"It was the Zeta Ray," Edward explained.

"You're afraid of the Zeta Ray?" Delores asked incredulously.

"Slime monsters know no fear," Edward insisted. "Mostly, we know slime. But still, there is something I cannot place my incredibly slippery finger on, something about that Zeta Ray, and *the Change*—"

Edward's voice faltered, as if, despite his protestations, there were certain things even slime monsters didn't want to think about.

Delores was once again aware of sounds in the darkness. The screams redoubled, even more bloodcurdling than before. And this time they were accompanied by other, softer noises, like the tearing of cloth, the rending of flesh, the splintering of bone, and the clacking of long and pointed teeth—almost as if, Delores reflected, something was being eaten alive.

Delores decided she didn't want to reflect any more.

"We may not have long before the Change starts all over again," Edward continued, as if he had finally found the courage to say what was in his heart, or whatever similar organ beat within the Slime Monster's breast. "And once the Change begins, who knows what is next? No, we must be married as soon as possible. And then, of course, there's the honeymoon to consider. And what about the china and silver patterns?" The monster sighed. "So much to do, so little time."

China and silver patterns? Delores also decided to put any thoughts of marriage to a thing made of muck out of her mind. She'd never get out of here if she descended into despair.

Instead, she asked the first question that had come into her head upon her arrival in this dreadful place.

"But—why here?"

"Here?" Edward's voice sounded surprised, almost shocked. "Where else could we go? This is home."

"Home?" Delores asked between the now-faltering screams. "You call a dark, foul-smelling, noisy and dangerous place like this—home?"

"Yes, it is rather pleasant, isn't it?" Edward agreed. "But I sense you are not entirely happy with our new surroundings. Probably has something to do with you being used to sunshine, and all those other nasty bright lights." Edward sighed. "It is true, you could not know this place the way I do."

The screams ended, and the roaring began again.

"I don't think I want to," Delores admitted.

"If you had only grown up here," Edward insisted, "the way I did. Oh, what happy childhood memories, rooting in the muck for Tremendofly maggots! You should try them. They're especially tasty, you know, just before they molt."

Tremendofly maggots? Despite her best efforts, Delores could feel despair seeping into her soul.

"Now I know I don't want to," she replied sullenly.

Edward made a wet *tsking* sound with what passed for his mouth. "My dear Delores, if only you'd give the place a chance. There is beauty here, all around us even now, in the cry of the dying Razorbird, and the grumbling song of the Gigantasaur as it rends and tears its evening meal. Or, if you listen carefully, you can hear the musical bubbling of the distant phosphorescent swamp as it claims another victim."

Now that Edward mentioned it, she did think she heard a distant bubbling noise, accompanied by the ever-present distant screams. None of this was making Delores feel any better. She had to get out of here—somehow, anyhow. "Uh, Edward? Could we go somewhere else and talk about this?"

"Too much, too soon, huh?" the muck-thing replied, sounding genuinely apologetic. "Maybe I should have waited to bring you home. We slime monsters were always impetuous. I'm sure it has something to do with our slippery constitution." Edward chuckled. "Oh, we're going to have such a wonderful life together. Why, I think we've just had our first domestic quarrel."

The monster took Delores' shoulder in his slimy yet firm grip. "Away we go," he whispered close by her ear. She had to struggle not to choke on his fetid breath. ''To someplace that isn't quite so picturesque.''

So, even though they would get away from here, she was still trapped in the Slime Monster's embrace. But she had to remind herself that, even now, she wasn't alone. Roger Gordon, the man she loved, had been chosen as the new Captain Crusader. Surely, a man of Captain Crusader's stature would have to have tremendous resources. Surely, Roger and their other allies could save her—somehow.

Edward's grip tightened.

''Keep watching the skies!'' the Slime Monster yelled.

There was a small explosion. Had there been any light here at all, Delores was sure she would have seen blue smoke.

''Roger!'' she called out to the void.

''Delores!'' Roger whispered as he stared at the sand.

''So,'' Zabana, Prince of the Jungle, asked over his shoulder. ''What we do now?''

''Uh—'' Roger replied. It was a good question, what with all that had happened, first with his mother, and then with Delores. But Roger had no answers.

''Uh—'' he added.

''But we must act!'' Zabana insisted. ''Fate of Cineverse at stake!''

''Arf arf!'' the police dog at Zabana's side added. ''Arf bark!''

''Dwight the Wonder Dog agrees,'' the rather short Big Louie translated. ''The jungle prince has a point. Now that the insidious Doctor Dread has made it clear that he and his minions are working to once more bring about the Change—''

Roger couldn't help himself. ''Dwight said all that?'' he asked.

''Zabana lose whole family to Change,'' the jungle prince agreed morosely. ''Wife Shirley go into real estate, son Son start own movie series. Even my faithful orangutang companion, Oogie—'' Zabana choked, unable to continue.

Yes, Roger remembered the Change, too—fifteen or twenty years ago, now—a time when movies lost their heroes, when the bad guys won, the good guys died, and boy didn't even get to meet girl. At the time, Roger thought movies might simply be mirroring the social unrest of the late sixties and early seventies. Now, though, he knew it was all because of the fiendish plans of Doctor Dread!

"Yes, the Change," Big Louie continued, "which, if it is allowed to again take control will mean the triumph of Doctor Dread, and the end of the Cineverse as we know it. Only Captain Crusader stands in the way of this awful catastrophe, our own Captain Crusader, Roger Gordon, lately of Earth, appointed by the Plotmaster to lead the forces of good in a last-ditch effort to rid the many cinematic worlds of Dread's evil!"

"That putsh it all together niceshly," the reformed drunkard Doc—still suffering from a slight case of sunstroke—slurred.

"I'll say, boyo," Officer O'Clanrahan agreed. "That's one of the most professional summaries I've ever heard. By all the saints, we could have used you on the force!"

"I'm a sidekick," Louie replied matter-of-factly. "Plot summaries are part of my job. You know, whatever moves the plot along."

And Roger realized the plot had to get moving, soon. He heard the sound of tuning guitars on the makeshift stage the surfers had set up on the beach. That meant it was almost time for more beach-party music. And music had a special power in the Cineverse—movie magic, Louie called it—a musical power that could make you want to spend the rest of your life in this seaside paradise. Bix Bale and the Belltones—with their red- and white-striped shirts and modified Beatle haircuts—would soon play yet another song extolling the virtues of sun, sand, and surfing, with perhaps some references to blond beach bunnies thrown in. And, once the music really started, all plans would be forgotten as everyone began to dance!

Roger wasn't as afraid of the power of movie magic as

he had been. He had, after all, conquered that great wave, the Cowabungamunga, through his own use of surfing song. But there was no time to delay, and—once the music began—there was no way to tell how long the surfing beat's subversive force might keep them under its sway. He had to use the Captain Crusader Decoder Ring he clutched in his hand to get his allies out of here. But where should they go next? Shouldn't somebody who'd been appointed Captain Crusader know this sort of thing?

And, besides that, one of the surfers was running straight toward him.

"Roger Dodger!" Brian called. His usual, creaseless surfer's face was wrinkled by a frown. "Something's going wrong! It's Frankie!"

He pointed to the stage.

"Oh, no," Big Louie added in horror. "Not this. Anything but this!"

Roger's mouth opened as he turned to the stage. Bix Bale and the Belltones had changed. They no longer sported the surfer look. Instead, their dark hair was cut and plastered to their heads, and they wore white polyester suits, with dark ruffled shirts open to the navel to reveal the dozens of gold chains that crisscrossed their chests. And their former surfing buddy Frankie—dressed just like the band—strode in front of them.

Roger had seen all of this someplace before.

"Frankie!" Brian insisted. "You can't do this, Frankie!"

"Hit it guys!" Frankie called in reply.

The music was different, only vaguely rock and roll. Oh, not that there wasn't a drumbeat. No, the drum was much louder than Roger had ever heard it in surf songs. It was right up in front of the music, very heavy, and very regular, almost too regular, as if the beat were being produced by a machine.

The music swelled. All Roger could see was the four-piece rock band. Where were those violins coming from, anyway?

Then Frankie started to sing.

"Don't you get in my way, girl,

"Oh, I've got to boogie,
Got to shake my thing,
Don't you get in my way, girl,
I'm a disco king!"

Everyone stared at the stage. For the moment, at least, there was no movie magic. The new music was too different, too far from the beach. But everybody knew what this new music meant.

"It'sh the Change!" Doc wailed for all of them.

Roger never thought it would be as bad as this.

3

Menge led the way into the secret headquarters.

"This is also known as the Citadel of Dread," he said softly to Mrs. G. as the great double doors slammed shut behind them, "although I think we may be changing the name soon—say, to the 'Stronghold of the Merciless'?"

Mrs. Gordon smiled at her man's confidence. Of course, why someone would want to take over a place as dreary as this was beyond her. The gray motif of the building's massive exterior carried over to the rather large interior as well. There was nothing inside but featureless gray walls and impossibly high ceilings. And all these shadows just had to go!

What this place needed, Mrs. G. decided, was a woman's touch. Say, an attractive floral arrangement here under that sputtering torch, and perhaps a series of colorful throw rugs along that endless hallway over there—little changes like that could do real wonders for the place. Once Mengy was in control around here, she could really brighten this secret headquarters up—make it into the sort of place you wouldn't be ashamed to invite the neighbors. If, she reflected, a place like this had any neighbors.

"You have a new life before you, Mrs. G.," Menge continued in that same soft, but urgent, tone as he led her through the never-ending corridors. "We *both* have new lives before us." He chuckled knowingly as he squeezed her hand. "You are a part of a new world, Antoinette. You should have a new identity that fits your new world."

"A new identity?" she replied uncertainly. What did he mean by that? Something, perhaps, like one of those makeovers she was always reading about in the fashion magazines. Reading, she reminded herself, but never doing.

"Yes!" Menge insisted. "Consider it, Mrs. G. Who, in your deepest, darkest heart, have you always wanted to be?"

"Well," she answered uncertainly, "I've never really thought about it." Her hands smoothed her floral print dress. "Until now, I've been happy with Mrs. Roger Gordon, Sr., homemaker."

But Menge shook his head firmly. "Absolutely not. That will never do for the most powerful woman in the Cineverse." He clutched her hand even more tightly than before. "For, now that you are at my side, you will be *very* powerful."

He stopped abruptly.

"Perhaps we shall find what we need in here."

He opened a door to his left marked WARDROBE. Mrs. G. followed him inside.

What she saw next took her breath away. The room was full of clothing, but not simply any clothing. She had seldom seen so many clothes in one place, and never in such variety—rack after rack of every shade and style imaginable. And, what's more, with the vast array of wild colors and jungle prints, fur collars, and metal studs, none of these clothes could be called understated. It was all rather like walking into the world's largest closet—or, at the very least, a very large discount department store.

She studied the nearest rack, and noticed a preponderance of snakeskin. She ran her fingers along one of the bumpy cowls.

Menge took her hand again and gently pulled it away. "That stuff's reserved for the boss. You can't wear it—just yet. Still, there's plenty left over for the well-dressed villain. Or villainess."

He walked down to the next rack, pulling her along. He frowned at a selection of hooded robes in black and white, purple and green, some in solid colors, others with images of spiders, tigers, vultures, and suchlike sewn onto the headpieces.

"Too plain," Menge murmured. "Wouldn't do you justice." He passed over a shelf of mystic turbans and similar headgear, many of them set with semiprecious stones, then dismissed another rack featuring a selection of metal-studded, see-through bikinis as "not your style."

He grinned before he even touched the third rack.

"Here it is!" he declared as he yanked a hanger free from its fellows. "The very thing!" He winked jauntily as he handed the clothing—something, she noticed approvingly, in basic black—to Mrs. G.

She took the costume and opened a door labeled CHANGING ROOM.

"Oh, don't forget these!" Mengy called after her. He passed a pair of boots to her through the still-open doorway. The boots were also basic black. Apparently, Mrs. G. thought, they were going for a total look.

She told Mengy he'd have to be patient and shut the door.

The dress was a bit tighter than she was used to. Still, she had been careful to keep her figure, and the dark color was very flattering, especially with her newly blond hair. Of course, she wasn't at all sure how practical this costume would be. Wouldn't black leather get awfully hot in the summer? But everything was in her size, even the boots, almost as if it had been made for her. And the accessories—those small silver skull earrings were quite darling in their way. Then there was the whip. She flicked the handle tentatively. The whip snapped smartly.

CRACK

She flipped the handle the other way.

CRACK snapped the whip again. She flipped her wrist back and forth. *CRACK CRACK CRACK* It was all so easy, the snapping leather almost an extension of her arm—like she had been handling a bullwhip all her life.

She was quite startled by the change when she looked in the full-length mirror. Part of her wanted to back away from anything this different, this bold, but another part of her wanted to giggle—no, she wanted to laugh out loud, long and strong—a laugh of total triumph.

Her clothes were no longer those of the everyday housewife. These were clothes of power.

She opened the door and stepped out to show the outfit to her Mengy.

Her man made a sound that was half gasp, half moan.

"It is *you*," he whispered, his face as full of wonder as a ten-year-old boy. "I never dreamed it would be this perfect."

"Do you really think so?" Mrs G. asked. Still, she couldn't help but smile.

"That, and more so," Mengy assured her. "You are no longer Mrs. Roger Gordon, Sr. You are now someone far better. You are"—he paused, searching for exactly the right words—"Mother Antoinette, Mistress of Evil!"

"Really?" Mrs. G. replied, still not quite convinced. She did like the sound of the first part of that—Mother Antoinette. But "Mistress" of Evil? Shouldn't it be "Matron of Evil"? She had been married, after all.

Still, why should she worry about such inconsequential details when the crack of that whip was so very satisfying?

"Yes," Menge answered throatily, his hand trembling close to her leather-clad shoulder. "It suits you surprisingly well." His small mouth worked silently for a moment beneath his pencil-thin mustache, as if he were having difficulty with what he wanted to say next. "And more than that," he added at last, "Antoinette, I—"

"Menge!" the nasal and irritating voice of Doctor Dread interrupted them.

Menge snapped to attention. "Yessir!" he shouted to the wall. Mrs. G. turned to look in the direction her man was facing, and was surprised to see a large, moving image covering the top half of that side of the room, rather like a gigantic television screen.

"What is"—Dread hesitated angrily—"keeping you?"

"Just some minor alterations," Menge assured that nasty Dread person. "I thought it appropriate to get our new recruit some more suitable attire."

"More"—Dread paused most unpleasantly—"suitable?

I decide what is *suitable* around here. Are you forgetting who is the authority on this world, in this Cineverse, who has the power to *deal* with people who displease him? I warn you, Menge—''

Mrs. G. had had enough of Dread's browbeating the man she loved. She stepped in front of the screen and flicked her wrist.

CRACK

''This is''—Dread hesitated in disbelief—''Mrs. Gordon?''

Mrs. G. smiled ever so slightly as she stared defiantly at Dread's image.

''Yes!'' Menge added hurriedly. ''But she is no longer simply Mrs. Gordon. She is now Mother Antoinette, Mistress of Evil!''

CRACK the new Mother Antoinette added, flicking the bullwhip at the screen. *CRACK CRACK CRACK*

Dread's mouth fell open.

''Yes, I suppose that is''—he hesitated, as if even the soon-to-be Master of the Cineverse might be at a loss for words—''quite suitable.''

Mother Antoinette smiled and snapped the whip.

Dread hastily broke the connection.

Menge put his hand on her shoulder. ''That was wonderful, Mrs. G.!''

She turned to look at him. His hand fell away.

''I mean, Mother Antoinette,'' he amended hastily. ''But we must go to the throne room. It is not yet time to make our move.''

It might have been her imagination, but Mrs. G. could have sworn Mr. M. was trembling as she walked past him, her three-inch heels clacking on the fortress floor.

The whip made small, snapping sounds as she idly toyed with it. Mengy moaned softly behind her.

She turned to look at her man. He appeared smaller, now that she was wearing those heels. ''Mengy? Is something the matter?''

''Oh no,'' he insisted, although he was sweating profusely—unusual in a place as cold and clammy as this dull gray fortress. "Everything is"—he swallowed—"just fine."

"If you say so." She brushed her blond hair away from her face. It looked like Mengy's knees were wobbling with some regularity, almost as a response to her every action. "Shall we proceed?"

"Yes, Mother Antoinette," Menge replied hurriedly, averting his gaze as he ran past her for the door. "Whatever you say."

Now, what could be the matter with him? Mother Antoinette smiled slightly, cracking the whip behind her as she followed Mengy from the room.

Whatever his problems were, she had ways to find them out.

4

There was the usual blue smoke.

"I hope you like this somewhat better," the Slime Monster's dour tones cut through the smog.

Anything, Delores thought, had to be better than that last place. Still, if that last dark and dangerous world was the place the Slime Monster called *home*, where might he bring her next? She decided to reserve judgment on their new surroundings until the smoke cleared.

Rays of sunlight cut through the thick blue fog, burning the remaining mist away in only a few seconds. But where were they? They stood on a quiet, well kept street, surrounded by a series of neat little white-frame houses set on a series of immaculate green lawns. Like one of the nicer streets on Earth, Delores thought, only perhaps a bit too bright, a bit too quiet, a bit too perfect.

Delores shivered. Too bright? Too perfect? She hoped Edward hadn't brought her to one of those Musical Comedy worlds. The surfing world had been seductive enough. If they had landed in one of those places where everyone was going to the fair or were on the verge of celebrating some major holiday in song, Delores and the monster might be doomed to stay here forever. Could that be what Edward truly wanted?

But Delores heard no distant orchestras or vocal choirs or hordes of tapping feet—none of the telltale signs of musical comedy. Instead, she could hear only birds chirping in the gentle breeze, and kids laughing as they rode their bikes in the suburban sunshine.

"Walk this way," Edward instructed, shambling quickly down the street.

If I could walk that way—Delores stopped herself. This was no time for comedy of any kind. She watched the tall, greenish-brown creature shuffle down the street before her, and realized that this was the first time she had seen the Slime Monster in the bright sunlight—the first time, in fact, she had seen the monster not hidden by shadow or covered with sand.

The creature was definitely humanoid, if somewhat on the large size, with appendages that approximated head, arms, and legs. And every inch of the monster's rather large frame was covered by a gooey, shining slime.

Except that the slime shone less with every second the Slime Monster stood in direct sunlight. Delores could see the muck already drying rapidly on Edward's back, cracking into patches like a mud flat too long deprived of rain. The widening cracks showed the slightest glimpse of something underneath—something of a much darker green and so highly polished that it glittered even more than the remaining slime, and flashed whenever the sunlight shone upon the cracks.

Was she glimpsing the actual skin under the monster's slime? Oddly enough, the texture beneath the mud reminded Delores of nothing so much as a rubber suit.

Edward groaned, a sound from deep inside, like the sunshine was not only drying his skin but his soul.

"Hurry!" he called to her. "There is little time!"

She had been right, then—Edward was drying out in the bright light. The monster couldn't live long under the direct sun. And he had come to this place because of Delores. What a sacrifice he must be making for her! For the first time, Delores felt the slightest twinge of compassion for this disgusting creature. She ran to follow him, careful to sidestep the still damp and malodorous trail Edward had left in his wake.

He breathed heavily, the air rasping in and out of his throat as the slime on his face dried enough for Delores to make out the outline of a nose and a pair of ears. Even a thin slit opened where the monster's mouth should be. And, as he dried, his rapidly shuffling gait became slower and slower.

So the Slime Monster wasn't as invincible as he had first appeared. Delores realized that if she could only expose the Slime Monster to enough heat and light, she might be rid of him forever.

Still, she wished it wouldn't have to come to that. There was something about this rapidly drying but still foul-smelling creature that was—well, perhaps "endearing" was too strong a word—but the fellow was certainly likable, and generally well-meaning, at least as monsters went. Delores sighed. There had to be some other way, short of the creature's total destruction, to say no to a slime monster.

"Almost there," Edward urged, his voice now little more than a whisper. When he looked at her, the muck drying on his head gave his face a look that might almost pass for tenderness.

Edward turned and hurried up the walk to one of the houses, a structure somewhat bigger than the other homes on the block, but of the same white-painted wood, with the same manicured green lawn.

Delores noticed that this place had a plaque by the door:

THE SOUTHERN CALIFORNIA INSTITUTE
OF
VERY ADVANCED SCIENCE

"If they can't help us," Edward croaked with another fond look in Delores' direction, "no one can."

And with that, the Slime Monster kicked down the door.

"Who's that?" an astonished guard yelled through a hole where a moment before the door, and a fair amount of the surrounding doorway, had stood.

"Pardon us," Edward mumbled as he made his faltering way over to a water fountain opposite the guard's station. He pressed the fountain's foot pedal with one mud-encrusted appendage, and drank.

And, as he drank, the mud turned back to slime with

astonishing speed. In mere seconds, Edward was back to his gooey, disgusting self.

"It's the Slime Monster!" the guard exclaimed. "Sound the alarm! Close down the—*glub*!"

"Sorry," Edward remarked as a stream of slime shot from the end of both his arms to engulf the guard. "But any of those options would be inconvenient."

He turned to Delores, who stared past the monster at the slime-covered guard. Then again, she considered, how did you relate to someone who shoots sludge for a living?

"Do you like it?" the monster asked, almost pathetically eager.

"Um—" Delores replied, still somewhat overcome by the course of events. "Like what?"

"My latest work." Edward pointed back to the pile of gray sludge where the uniformed guard had blubbered only a moment before. "I call it 'Security Guard, Covered by Slime.'"

"Uh—" Delores answered as truthfully as possible, considering the circumstances, "this is all a little new to me."

"Oh, dear, I've worried about this so." Edward fretted. "Isn't my work accessible enough? Now, now, don't tell me. It's the title, isn't it? It lacks that certain ambiguity so important in modern art! I've always been too direct, you know. It's an occupational hazard, when you're a monster." He paused for an instant, then added, "Perhaps I should call it something like 'Security Number Thirty-four.' What do you think?"

Delores didn't know what to say. Most of her wanted to say "LET ME OUT OF HERE!" She had to admit, there was nothing like a new pile of stinking sludge to remind her she was being chaperoned by a slime monster—the same monster who, no matter how polite he appeared, was holding her against her will.

"It's not the title, is it?" Edward answered himself, his voice grim, as if his worst fears had been realized. Slime flew about the room as he ruefully shook his head. "It's the work itself! Now, now, no misdirected kindness. You can tell me. What do you *really* think? I may be slippery, but I can take it!''

What could you say, Delores considered, when the subject in question was a totally disgusting mound of gray sludge? Still, whatever his other failings, the monster had been unerringly polite in her presence. Perhaps, if she could be as polite in turn, she could somehow talk this monster out of the whole wedding thing.

But what *did* she really think?

''Uh, no,'' she began, doing her best not to hurt the monster's feelings. ''It's actually quite . . .'' Her voice drifted off as her mind failed to conjure up any way to finish the sentence.

''Perhaps I need to add a little something?'' Edward prompted, still eager to please.

''Something to—the slime?'' Delores asked, hard pressed not to shiver at the very thought.

''Well, yes, that's a possibility—'' Edward added thoughtfully. ''I *was* adding sand to the slime back on the beach. The whole thing hardened quite nicely. But I was thinking of pursuing something not quite so physical—'' To illustrate his meaning he pointed skyward, with an object that might have been a finger. ''Something, instead, that would reveal my more sensitive aspects; something to make this more of a total aesthetic experience.''

''Total aesthetic—'' Delores began. Politeness, after all, could only go so far.

But Edward had become so excited by this latest concept that he didn't even hear her.

''That's it!'' he cried. ''I need a context for my slime, something that everyday people—some of whom perhaps have never even met a slime monster—can relate to in their everyday, slime-monsterless lives. But''—the monster hesitated, grappling with this new concept—''what would be best? Perhaps some sort of dramatic emphasis, even—dare I say it?—poetry!''

''Poetry?'' Delores asked, helpless to do anything else.

Edward's slimy face showed an even more faraway look

than usual. "Poetry. Perhaps something like"—the monster cleared whatever passed for his throat. " 'Don't take it hard that I've covered the guard. I know what is mine and it's got to be slime'—that sort of thing?"

Edward glanced at Delores' look of dismay, and sighed. "Still, it lacks resonance, doesn't it? If only slime was more of a universal experience!"

"Hey, there he is!" somebody yelled.

"He got Sweeney!" a second voice added.

Two more guards ran into the foyer of the institute. Before Delores could even react, Edward promptly covered both of them with sludge.

"Of course," the monster added, "the longer we stand here, the more universal the slime experience becomes." He paused to regard his latest creation. "There it is, my new, improved creation. 'Three Security Guards, Covered by Slime.' Or should it be 'Security Number Thirty-five?' " He glanced at Delores. "Still not universal, huh? Where have I gone wrong?"

Delores decided that she had taken politeness as far as it could go, especially with that rank odor coming from the muck-covered guards. She looked up at Edward.

"Couldn't you do something else other than cover people with slime?"

The room shook as the Slime Monster roared. Had Delores gone too far?

Edward took a ragged breath, clenching those two objects that might have been fists as he brought himself under control. Still quaking with emotion, he turned to regard Delores. She thought she saw two tiny points of ruby light where his eyes should be, twin coals glowing in his slime-enshrouded face.

"Why—" he rumbled, "are artists always so misunderstood?" He placed what passed for a hand in front of what passed for a face.

"There must be something I can do!" the monster continued, his voice once again quiet, yet dour and determined. "Say—I could read the phone book backwards, thus expressing my reaction to the emptiness of present-day society."

A fellow in a white lab coat emerged from a door off the foyer. Edward covered the newcomer in sludge before he could finish his scream. Delores turned away.

"Or I could paint myself in decorator colors," the monster continued, "thus commenting cleverly on the folly of modern home-furnishings."

A half-dozen security guards ran yelling from two opposite corridors, their pistols drawn. Delores made a gagging noise as Edward drowned them all in slime.

"Or I could even cover myself with hot fudge sauce, whipped cream, and a maraschino cherry," the monster further mused, "thus critiquing the arbitrary nature of the food chain and my place within it."

Edward paused, as if waiting for a response, but Delores—with all her attention diverted to controlling her gag response—had long ago given up trying to keep up her end of the conversation. A voice screamed in her head: *Let me out of here!*

The Slime Monster looked uncertainly down at his feet. "Then again, I could learn to tap dance."

They were interrupted by the sound of sirens, distant at first, but becoming much louder before they stopped abruptly.

"ALL RIGHT, MONSTER!" a bullhorn-amplified voice shouted outside. "WE KNOW YOU'RE IN THERE!"

Edward lifted what passed for his head up to the heavens. "Why does this always have to happen? 'ALL RIGHT, MONSTER! WE KNOW YOU'RE IN THERE!' Can't the forces of law and order ever have any originality? Is there no place in the Cineverse for an artist like me?" The monster shook his head ruefully. "Well, perhaps there will be, after our experiment."

Our experiment? Delores didn't like the sound of that. *Let me out of here—now!*

"SEND OUT THE GIRL AND WE'LL GO EASY ON YOU!" the bullhorn voice continued.

"Send out the girl?" Edward despaired. "Come on guys, show a little originality." He waved to Delores. "Come with me"—he paused as ominously as Doctor Dread—"unless you want to see the entire police force covered with slime." He glanced back toward the front door. "At least those guys haven't said anything about having the building surrounded—"

"WE'RE WARNING YOU, MONSTER!" the bullhorn responded promptly. "WE HAVE THE ENTIRE BUILDING SURROUNDED!"

"We really do have to leave now," Edward insisted. He shooed her down the central corridor in front of him. "I sense some resistance on your part." He quickly lumbered after her. "But I trust this institute has the proper tools to make us more compatible."

More compatible? Delores shivered. What did he mean—psychological programming to make her more accepting of slime? Her throat was almost too dry for her to swallow. Maybe she'd have to leave Edward out in the noonday sun after all.

The Slime Monster was almost on top of her. Delores hurried down the hall, past door after neatly labeled door:

MINIATURIZATION LAB

OUTER SPACE COMMUNICATIONS ROOM

GIANT BRAIN EXPERIMENT

"Turn here," Edward instructed, pointing past a door marked CENTER FOR PHENOMENAL GROWTH. What, Delores wondered, could Edward want down here? She was relieved when they passed the door marked ATOM SMASHER; doubly relieved as they passed the ALIEN PARASITE HOSPITALITY SUITE.

"Stop," Edward commanded.

Delores stopped.

The slime monster opened a door marked TRANSMOGRIFIER.

"After you," he intoned.

Delores hesitated. How could she get out of here?

"You have no choice," the Slime Monster insisted. "This is your destiny."

It was either this, Delores realized, or being covered by slime.

She took a step into the darkened room.

5

"Hey!"

It was Big Louie's voice, yelling through the smoke. Loads and loads of thick, blue smoke.

At first, Roger thought someone new had arrived on the Beach-Party-turned-Disco world.

But then he realized the disco beat had faded away, lost beneath the sound of a distant wind. And there was too much smoke—the kind of smoke that only appeared when you were traveling between worlds.

They had left the Beach Party planet behind. But wasn't he the one with the ring that transported them between those worlds? And he hadn't touched it—had he? And he couldn't remember anybody saying "See you in the funny papers!"

Then his feet were on solid ground again. They were somewhere new. But how?—where?—and why?

"What's going on here?" Louie asked loudly, once again voicing the disquiet of the entire group.

"This sort of thing is enough to make a fella sober," Doc agreed, apparently startled out of the effects of his sunstroke by the sudden change of scene.

Roger had to admit that the adrenalin was pounding in his veins as well, in part because of that music he heard coming from outside the blue cloud. And it was very urgent music.

"Faith and begorrah!" Officer O'Clanrahan added.

"Yip bark arf!" Dwight added with a concerned bark.

"Listen!" Roger insisted. The music was getting louder, relentless horns pounding over constant violins, as if the hidden orchestra was urging Roger to do—what?

"You hear something?" the Prince of the Jungle asked

incredulously. "Even Zabana, with his jungle-bred senses able to hear slithering of slug at six hundred paces, hear nothing but distant wind." The jungle prince paused. "That, and—now I listen—even more distant growl of engines."

Nothing but the distant growl of engines? But the music was so obvious!

"You can't hear this?" Roger found he had to shout over the pounding of the kettledrum. "Not the horns or the violins? Even that incessant drum?"

The smoke chose that instant to clear.

They were on some inner-city street, in what looked like an industrial section of some town, with large warehouses on either side, and the crumbling remains of elevated trolley tracks overhead.

That was it. There was no orchestra anywhere in sight. Paradoxically, the music grew even louder, a swirl of woodwinds adding punch to the horns. Roger wondered if the orchestra was hiding in one of the warehouses.

"Now, Roger," Louie asked, "exactly what were we listening—"

"Bark bark yip!" Dwight the Wonder Dog interrupted.

Big Louie looked in the direction the dog indicated.

"Oh, no!" he groaned.

"What matter?" Zabana asked as he hunkered into a defensive jungle crouch. "Is Change?"

"Worse than that," Big Louie answered. "The Change has been here and gone. Don't you see what's coming towards us? It's a car chase!"

The music ceased abruptly as those distant engines Zabana had heard—and the cars those engines were attached to—got much, much closer, very, very fast.

"And they're coming right for us!" screamed Louie, with his astonishing ability to encapsulate the obvious. "And there's nowhere to hide!"

Roger took a closer look at their surroundings. They had materialized in the exact middle of the broad avenue, and the warehouses to either side were long, featureless brick buildings, with only a distant garage door and a few trash cans to break the monotony.

So Big Louie was right. There wasn't much of anyplace to go. For some reason, though, Roger didn't think it was hopeless. For one thing, he was supposed to be Captain Crusader now. And Captain Crusader never gave up!

Besides, Roger knew his movies. And, as long as he thought like a movie, how could he help but win?

The cars would reach them in a matter of seconds, a dry-cleaning van pursued by a dented yellow Chevy. But didn't cars in car chases, when they were about to run into innocent bystanders, swerve out of the way at the last possible second? Of course they did. Roger had seen it happen in movie chase after movie chase.

The cars headed straight for them.

The vehicles swerved—Roger now remembered—unless one of the cars was being driven by the bad guys.

Then they were in trouble. Bad guys, after all, liked to run over people.

He recognized the driver in the dry-cleaning van. It was Professor Peril—one of Doctor Dread's evil henchpeople!

Peril grinned as he bore down on Roger and his fellows. The van's engines growled as it's evil driver floored the gas pedal.

And Roger realized what they had to do.

"Quick!" He yelled to the others. "Follow me!"

He sprinted past the rusted elevated train support, straight for the row of trash cans. He could hear the others running behind him and, beyond them, much too close, the roar of a dry-cleaning van.

Roger ran past the garbage. He stopped and turned when he reached the neverending brick wall.

"What's the matter, boyo?" Officer O'Clanrahan asked between gasps for breath. "You can't stop us here. We'll be sitting ducks!"

"No," Roger replied tersely. "If I'm right, there's no better place for us than right here."

The van bore down on them, barely missing the rusted

metal support pole as the tires squealed into a final, deadly turn. The vehicle was so close that Roger could see Professor Peril laugh silently and economically on the other side of the windshield. But Peril's look of triumph turned to one of horror as the car swerved out of his control to hit the garbage cans.

"Of course!" Big Louie exclaimed. "Cars in car chases always hit something—if they can, they hit something made of metal, something that makes a lot of noise. And what makes more noise than a garbage can? Brilliant!"

Roger was just happy that his ploy had worked. He had remembered the propensity for cars to run into things. He hoped that same propensity had been universal enough to be one of the Laws of the Cineverse. And it was!

"Curse you, Captain Crusader!" Peril shouted from behind his half-open passenger window. "I haven't forgotten what you did to Mort the Killer Robot and Diablo, the Gorilla with the Mind of a Man. I will wreak my revenge—" He frowned as he saw the rapidly approaching yellow Chevy.

"—eventually," he concluded as he threw the van into reverse, and, once clear of the garbage cans, careened forward down the street.

The dented Chevy screeched to a halt in front of Roger.

Two fellows in rumpled pastel suits opened doors on either side of the car. The driver had a three-day growth of beard, and the other guy wore an earring.

"Cops." Three-day-growth flipped open a billfold to reveal a badge. "You folks okay?"

Roger glanced around at his band. They all appeared to have escaped unscathed.

"Good," Three-day-growth replied before Roger had a chance to answer. "Then you won't mind answering a few questions."

"Yeah," Earring interjected. "We saw the way that van went after you. What's your connection to Professor Peril?"

"Our connection?" Roger asked incredulously. "He tried

to run us over! He's our enemy. I mean, he's a bad guy, isn't he?"

"So you say," Earring replied, unconvinced. "What do you think, Frank? Should we take them down to the station?"

Oh, no, Roger thought. *Down to the station*? They had a Cineverse to save! They didn't have time to become involved in the everyday plot of another movie world. Somehow, he had to get his friends out of this particular plot before things got any more complicated. But Roger had learned from experience—and a few close calls on unfriendly movie worlds—that you didn't use your Captain Crusader Decoder Ring to escape unless you knew exactly where you were going. If Roger was going to extricate them from their present difficulty, he would have to use his wits.

Louie jumped in before Roger could say anything. "You can't pin a thing on us, coppers!" he yelled. "What's the charge?"

"Louie!" Roger called. Louie replied with a helpless shrug. The sidekick had come from a *Film Noir* world, hadn't he? He probably had to talk back to the cops in exactly that way—it sounded like another Law of the Cineverse.

"Arf, arf, bark!" Dwight insisted.

"Oh, yeah?" Earring growled. "Does that dog have a license?"

"Dog not need license," Zabana insisted. "That Dwight the Wonder Dog!"

"Really?" Three-day-growth murmured. "I *thought* that mutt looked familiar."

But Earring wasn't impressed. He pointed a finger at the jungle prince. "You—I wouldn't talk. You're violating Municipal Statute Seven-O-One-Seven—wearing a loincloth within city limits."

"Hey, boyos!" Officer O'Clanrahan interjected. "I've spent too many years on the force to put up with this. Begorrah! It's harassment, plain and simple. Cops don't do that sort of thing where I come from."

"Where you come from?" Earring smirked as he turned to O'Clanrahan. "Hey, look at this guy! And who are you pretending to be? The police haven't worn that kind of uniform for twenty years. And, buddy, you'd better lose the brogue—"

"Now," Doc drawled, "I think we've gone a little bit too far here." He softly patted the pocket of his double-breasted suit, where he kept his six-shooter.

Both of the rumpled cops went for their guns.

Roger felt somebody tug on his sleeve. He glanced around to see a very anxious Big Louie. "Can't you see what's happening?" the sidekick whispered. "Cops fighting cops, heroes questioning heroes. The friction—everything about this confrontation—it's the Change!"

"The Change?" Roger repeated. He saw that Doc and Officer O'Clanrahan had drawn their guns as well. "What can we do?"

"There's only one thing we can do," Louie replied as he scowled grimly at their pastel-suited adversaries. "It's time for Captain Crusader to say something!"

Huh? Time for Captain Crusader to say something? Did Louie mean—

Doc took a step toward one of the cops. The other cop drew a bead on Officer O'Clanrahan. Roger realized Louie was right. He had to do it. It was up to Captain Crusader now.

Roger cleared his throat.

"Uh—" he began hesitantly. "The policeman is your friend."

Everyone turned to stare at Roger. Was it his imagination, or did they all seem a little less tense than they had before?

"Oh, yes," he added, a bit more quickly. "Always look both ways before you cross the street."

Yes! He definitely saw one of the cops relax his grip on his gun.

But the four men still faced each other, each side waiting for the other to make the first move. Trotting out tired old aphorisms, while it seemed to be a step in the right direction, simply wasn't getting the job done. Roger realized he needed something brand new, something that would capture the moment. Something, say, that covered tense situations.

Thanks in large part to years of training in public relations, he came up with that something almost immediately. And while it wasn't up there with such pithy Captain Crusader classics as "A clean plate is a happy plate," he hoped that it would do.

"How about this?" Roger ventured.

Everyone leaned toward Roger, the street silent save for a quiet but persistent patriotic tune on flute and drum.

It was now or never. Roger said it:

"Guns may come and guns may go, but a friend is a friend forever."

Both Earring and Three-day-growth reholstered their weapons.

Earring grinned at Roger. "Well, why didn't you say so in the first place?"

"We're always glad to help Captain Crusader," Three-day-growth agreed.

Earring laughed. "Still, that jogging outfit of yours had us fooled for a while. Most of your disguises are a bit fancier."

Roger might have to do something about his clothes. There were so many facets of Captain Crusader that he hadn't even considered! At least, Roger thought, he could try to keep his answer in character.

"I have to travel incognito," he replied solemnly. "These are dangerous times."

Both cops nodded, as if this was the only sort of answer they would expect. Roger really had convinced them he was the hero's hero, Captain Crusader. Now, if only he believed in that himself.

"But that man who was just here—" Roger added.

"Oh." Three-day-growth chuckled. "You mean the Professor."

So they knew about Peril already? That would make things a little easier. However they had arrived in this place, they now had a purpose. Professor Peril could lead them to Doctor Dread—and the heart of the Change!

"But how do we find this Professor?" Roger asked.

"Oh, don't worry about that," Three-day-growth reassured Roger. "That guy Peril has a thing about wasting time. He swore he was out to get you, didn't he? Well, with the Professor's efficiency, all you have to do is wait for a minute, and he'll confront you all over again."

"What that?" Zabana interrupted, cupping his jungle-bred ear to better hear the approaching noise. "Sound bigger than car." He paused, while his jungle-bred brain considered this information. "Maybe—very big car?"

Around the far corner of the left-hand warehouse came a very large cloud of dust—brown in color this time, rather than the Cineverse blue. And out of that dust came a very distinctive sound, sort of a roaring and clanking combined.

The music, after a final warning blast of horns, disappeared.

"Oh, shit," Earring shouted over the rapidly increasing clamor. "We'd better get reinforcements!"

Both of the cops jumped into their battered Chevy and drove away.

"What could make the cops run away?" Louie asked for everybody.

Dwight barked.

"No!" Louie shouted in reply. "It can't be!"

Roger didn't need to ask Louie to translate the Wonder Dog's remark. He could now see the shape of the vehicle through the dust.

It was more than a very large car.

Actually, it was a tank.

6

Menge scurried down yet another of the seemingly endless corridors. Antoinette confidently strode after him. It was amazing how quickly she had gotten used to walking in these spike heels, not to mention the comforting rustle of her leather skirt and the solid feel of the bullwhip in her hand.

"Almost there!" her little man called over his shoulder. He was puffing from the exertion. Antoinette had found the walk exhilarating, at least in part because these long halls had given her plenty of space to practice her whip technique. After only a few tries, she could snuff a sputtering torch at fifteen paces.

"Here we are!" Menge waved for her to follow him around yet another corner.

They faced another set of giant double doors, fully the equal of those that led into this fortress. And in front of these doors stood a pair of guards in dark uniforms, with automatic weapons at the ready.

"Halt!" the two guards shouted in unison. "What is your business with Dread?"

"Our business?" Menge bristled at the audacity of his inferiors. "You have no right to question our business. Make way for Mother Antoinette, Mistress of Evil!"

"Mother Antoinette?" one of the guards jeered back.

"We have no orders concerning any Mother—" the other guard began to scoff.

But Mother Antoinette had had enough of underlings. She flicked her wrist.

CRACK went her whip.

"Uh—" one of the guards answered with a nervous swallow.

"Er—" the other guard replied with a glance at his gun.

But the guards made no move away from the door. They apparently were still not convinced.

CRACK the whip argued. *CRACK CRACK CRACK*

The guards looked at each other.

"Make way for Mother Antoinette!" they chorused as they stepped aside and opened the giant doors.

Menge led the way into the great hall beyond. And it was a truly great hall, as large inside as the central courtyard of your average indoor mall. Unlike the rest of the colorless fortress, this room was decorated, with two rows of floor-to-ceiling wall-hangings running the length of the hall. Each tapestry depicted a different dramatic scene—if "dramatic" was the proper word to use. The tapestry just inside the door showed a man in a black hat shooting another man wearing white. In the next scene, a swarthy man in a stove-pipe hat laughed at the woman he had tied to the railroad tracks. Farther along the wall, Antoinette's gaze was drawn to a particularly graphic depiction of a giant reptile destroying an entire Oriental city. These tapestries were not simply dramatic, Mrs G. realized, they were dramatically evil, depiction after depiction of vileness triumphant.

And where did these two rows of wall-hangings lead? At the far end of the hall, beyond the last of the great tapestries, stood a huge chair, a dark, flat gray in color, as if it was made out of slate. And sitting in this uncomfortable chair was the man Antoinette recognized from the television screen in the wardrobe room. This was Doctor Dread.

Menge scrambled forward, with Mother Antoinette close at his heels.

The man on the throne looked up from the brightly colored cereal box he was studying. Even at this distance, Mother Antoinette could read the box's large, red label: NUT CRUNCHIES.

"What?" the enraged voice of Doctor Dread hesitated

portentously. "What is the meaning of this—intrusion?"

"I have brought Mrs. Gordon," Menge replied hurriedly as he continued to move forward. "Or Mother Antoinette," he amended as he glanced back to her, "as you ordered."

"What's that?" Dread barked as he tossed the cereal box behind the throne. He seemed to flinch slightly when he looked at Antoinette. "Why—so I did. But why didn't the guards—detain you? Why weren't you—properly announced?"

Menge and Antoinette stopped a dozen paces before the throne.

"The guards saw fit to let us pass," Mother Antoinette replied with the slightest of smiles. The whip quivered teasingly in her hand, not unlike a cobra ready to strike.

"What? What do you mean—" Dread hesitated as his gaze traveled up her whip and across her leather costume, until his eyes locked with her own.

"—Oh," he finished somewhat more quietly. "They did?" Dread broke away from her gaze to glance down at his snakeskin shoes.

"Who is the newcomer?" a woman's voice, surprisingly gruff, said from behind a jet-black curtain to the side of the throne.

"Ah, Bertha!" Dread called with surprising enthusiasm. "Why don't you come out here and—meet the newcomers?"

The heavy black drapes parted, and one of the largest women Antoinette had ever seen stepped into view. Not that she was fat. No, although there was substantial weight beneath the black vinyl jumpsuit she wore, it was firm, solid weight, like layer after layer of muscle. She was tall, too. Dread, even on his raised throne, seemed dwarfed by her presence.

"Big Bertha," Dread began solicitously. "I'd like you to meet Mrs. Ro—"

"No longer!" Menge interrupted with a shout. "This is Mother Antoinette! Mistress of Evil!"

"Yes," Dread added hurriedly, as if he wished to regain

some sort of control over the situation, "the woman who Menge has brought into our midst does indeed call herself—Mother Antoinette. She is also the—mother of Roger Gordon."

"*The* Roger Gordon?" Bertha asked as she crossed the room toward Antoinette.

"Yes." It actually embarrassed her a bit to admit this. "As unworthy as he is, Roger Gordon is"—it was her turn to hesitate—"my son."

Bertha smiled in a feral sort of way. "Oh, I wouldn't be that hard on poor Roger," she purred. She reached out and grabbed Antoinette's hand, shaking it heartily. "I always thought of your son as"—she paused to run her tongue over her teeth—"good breeding stock."

Mrs. G. frowned slightly at the look in Big Bertha's eyes. For the first time since she had picked up the whip, Mother Antoinette felt a twinge of pity for her son.

Bertha turned to throw a brightly colored box at the throne.

"Incidentally, Doctor, you dropped something."

The snakeskin-suited villain yelped as he grabbed the rectangular projectile. A handful of Nut Crunchies fell out before Doctor Dread could right the box.

"Careful!" he warned portentously. "These boxes do more than contain Captain Crusader Decoder Rings. They also hold"—he hesitated tellingly—"Captain Crusader's—secrets."

"Pardon me, O leader," Menge said as he took a step forward. "These brightly colored yellow and red cereal boxes contain"—he paused in a manner that would have done Dread credit—"secrets?"

"Are you too"—Dread sneered at his underling—"blind to see? This is why I am the leader, and you are the lackey! What better place to put them, than boldly on box after box of children's cereal!"

He turned the Nut Crunchies' package around in his pale hands. "Listen to these—messages that I have decoded from the back of the box: 'Social studies makes good citizens'. 'When riding your bike, always use hand signals!' How inane can you get? It *has* to be a code. No one could care about citizenship that much! What is the true—meaning of these phrases? Or could it be something—besides the message? Think on it!" He poked a clawlike forefinger at the side of the box. "Does anyone really know the true nature of—riboflavin?"

He looked out at those gathered around him, but none of them ventured a response.

"Exactly!" Dread cried, punching the Nut Crunchies box for emphasis. "There are so many possibilities, and all right under our noses. If only I could decipher Captain Crusader's true meaning."

Mother Antoinette considered Dread's dilemma. She herself had changed so much since taking up the whip that she might not be able to understand anything about a breakfast cereal box. "Perhaps," she ventured, "it is something that truly evil people cannot comprehend."

Dread tossed the box aside to glare down at her. "I comprehend—everything. Do not underestimate Doctor Dread! I demand respect!"

"Really?" Mother Antoinette smiled at that. "I could teach you a thing or two—about respect."

She flicked her wrist.

CRACK

Dread flinched as the whip snapped inches from his overly aristocratic nose.

"That's it!" Big Bertha encouraged. "Make them suffer!"

But Doctor Dread was not suffering. Instead, he stared at Mrs. G. with an even more single-minded intensity.

"Mother Antoinette," the archfiend began, hesitating longer than she had ever heard him hesitate. "I must say—I find you—interesting. Perhaps—at last—after years of search—I have found—a woman—after my—own heart."

"No!" Menge cried, running between Mrs. G. and the throne.

Dread turned his fiendish gaze to his underling.

"No?" he repeated in a voice that dripped with displeasure.

"I mean," Menge hastily amended, "she can be of so much use to us out in the Cineverse. There is no time for romance once the Change has begun."

But Menge's explanation only seemed to infuriate the villainous leader. "The Change? Who are you to tell me—"

This had gone far enough.

CRACK

Mother Antoinette interrupted them.

CRACK CRACK CRACK The whip danced between Menge and Dread, snapping with the warning regularity of a Barry Manilow dance number. Both men backed away from the dancing leather.

"Can't we talk about this?" Menge pleaded as he half turned to her. "Who got you that whip in the first place?"

CRACK

In a way, Mrs. G. was sorry she had to answer Mengy in this way, but there would be no better time to show her authority than right now. Her whip hand went wild.

CRACK CRACK Menge threw his arms up to protect his face. *CRACK CRACK CRACK* Dread cringed in his throne.

"Yes, yes, yes!" Big Bertha began to laugh as she slapped a black vinyl-coated knee. "Reduce these men to quivering rabbits!"

Somehow, Bertha's overheated enthusiasm caused Mother Antoinette's whip hand to hesitate. Dread grabbed the business end of the whip with his bare hand. "Bunnies?" he screamed, his fear turned to rage. "Never mention—bunnies!"

Mrs. G. tugged on the whip, but Dread still tightly held the other end. It was Mother Antoinette's turn to stare at the snakeskin-suited man upon the throne. Perhaps this Dread had some backbone after all.

The Doctor smiled slightly, and released his end of the whip, breaking the tension between them.

"So, Mother Antoinette," he said, his voice as smooth as a used-car dealer's. "You present some—interesting possibilities. I must—consider my options."

He pointed at the large woman by his side as he descended from the throne. "Bertha, I need your counsel. If you will follow me?" He paused before the black curtain. "And Mother Antoinette, I shall see you—and your whip—again."

"It was a pleasure meeting you, Mother Antoinette," Bertha added. "Someday, I plan to get to know your son"—she stopped for a moment to allow her ham-sized hands to run up and down her black-vinyl jumpsuit—"on a very close and personal level."

The large woman turned smartly and marched away, following Doctor Dread to whatever lay behind the curtain.

Mrs. G. stared for a long moment at the spot where Bertha disappeared, a troubled feeling stirring deep in the pit of her stomach—so troubled that, for a moment, she almost forgot her whip.

"Mother Antoinette," Menge whined by her side. "I must talk to you!"

"Yes, yes, Mengy. There's much we have to work on." She paused, staring thoughtfully at her man's bald pate. It would do her no harm to reveal some of her concerns to this underling—especially now that she knew he could become *her* underling. "But there is something I am curious about. What happens to the men Bertha chooses?"

"Oh, that," Menge replied with distaste, not quite suppressing a shudder. "You don't want to see them the next morning. They seem to age twenty or thirty years overnight."

"The next morning? I see." The answer did not seem encouraging. "And if they stay with her a second night?" Antoinette asked.

"Well, there's always the incinerator—the fortress here has a big one in the basement—" Menge shuddered outright this time. "Not that there's much left to burn."

Not much left to burn? Part of Antoinette told her it was

only what her son deserved; *that* would teach him never, ever to call. But there was another voice deep within her, barely decipherable, almost infinitesimally small, in fact—but a recognizable voice nonetheless, a voice unfazed by the Zeta Ray, which wanted to actually save her son.

Mother Antoinette found it all rather bothersome. She caressed the handle of her whip in an attempt to soothe her jangled nerves.

"It will be all right." Menge spoke by her elbow. "There is so much uncertainty, with the Change rushing toward us and all—"

Mother Antoinette snapped her whip reassuringly, cutting off her man's doubtful words. The Change, hmm? That was all Menge and Dread seemed to talk about, although she didn't think either one of them had really explained what they meant by that phrase. Not that it mattered much. With her new clothes and abilities, Mother Antoinette decided that she welcomed change.

She squeezed the shoulder of the man still quivering slightly by her side. She smiled to herself. As far as she was concerned, the changes had only just begun.

7

"No," Delores replied.

She could see the room beyond the open door, a room filled with dark and glistening machinery.

"No?" Edward asked, mildly surprised, she supposed, that anyone would contradict a slime monster.

Delores couldn't take her eyes from the room's interior.

The machinery was everywhere, covering walls and ceiling and all but a narrow walkway on the floor. The walkway led to two chairs, side by side, bathed in a harsh white light, almost too bright to stare at directly, and all the more startling for its sharp contrast to the dark but highly reflective metal all around. Tiny red lights flashed here and there, beckoning her inside. The lights were coldly beautiful against the oiled black steel, reminding her of nothing so much as sunlight glittering on a spider's web.

She realized that this room couldn't be any more of a trap if it were a spider's web—not really a room so much as a huge, mechanical entity, alive with tiny lights and a dozen different soft growls of motors at the ready. It waited for her, and when she stepped inside, she would be consumed—fuel for the great engine.

"No," she reiterated, looking away from the frigidly fascinating metal. "I am not going to follow you into something called a Transmogrifier."

"Fine," the Slime Monster replied as he shambled back from the door. "Then you go first."

Delores frowned. The monster was not getting the idea. But she had had enough. She had spent too many years in Hero School to play damsel in distress for very long, even to a slime monster. She should have declared her independence from Edward a long time ago. True, she had felt sorry for him, but that wasn't the sort of thing you could build a relationship on—even a monster/victim relationship. Delores' course was clear to her now. She had to declare her independence. There was no going back.

"No, Edward," she said, slowly and firmly. "There's nothing to keep me here. You can no longer sway me by threatening my friends. We've left my friends far behind. And your intentions, while sincere in their slime-covered way, are inappropriate, to say the least—especially now, when the very existence of the Cineverse is at stake!"

Edward roared, a sound that somehow combined the gurgle of a drain with the blare of an elephant. Delores decided she really didn't like the sound of that roar.

"Why must I be so misunder—" Edward interrupted himself. "Oh, I know. It's a Law of the Cineverse—me being a monster and all. But it certainly can get frustrating."

It was the Slime Monster's turn to stare inside at the great machine for a long, silent moment. The room hummed softly in anticipation.

"Perhaps," Edward continued, his voice flat, virtually without emotion, "some of my actions seem inappropriate, but you—of all people—must understand. I thought, with you, I might be happy. And how many chances for happiness does a slime monster have?"

The creature got a faraway look in the crimson-glowing apertures that could have been his eyes. "Perhaps, with you, even my art could take a happier turn." Something like a sigh escaped from something like a mouth. "Instead of adding sand to my slime, I might add flowers."

Delores shook her head. Here she was, starting to feel sorry for this muck-thing again. Actually, she was all for Edward's happiness, as long as that happiness didn't include her and a room full of highly experimental scientific gizmos. She decided she'd better get out of here now, before she ended up in that room with that machine.

But how could she get away from a creature who was so handy with slime? She could probably only run a few steps before the monster reacted. She needed a place to hide. But where? Perhaps the door across the way might hold the answer, the door marked EXPERIMENTAL ANIMAL LAB.

Delores still had to reckon with the speed of slime. She realized, to reach even a door as close as this, she would have to distract Edward first.

"Edward," she said as levelly as she could manage. "Let's be reasonable about this. Transmogrification? It sounds awfully dangerous."

"There's no turning back now," the monster insisted. "It is our only chance for happiness."

"But Edward!" It was very difficult to stamp your foot authoritatively when you were wearing the kind of high-fashion heels she had changed into on the *Film Noir* world. Still, Delores did her best. "I don't want that chance!"

But Edward was as firm as his body chemistry allowed. "I am sorry, but you have no choice. In this matter, I do have to be a monster. After transmogrification, we will both be different, and so much more compatible. Our very atoms shall intermingle, and we will share in a way most couples can only dream about. And after that? No longer will we have to limit ourselves to the reality of a single movie world. Once both of us are infused with the power of slime—the Cineverse will be ours! We will be able to explore whole new vistas—worlds beyond worlds beyond worlds—together." He waved what might have been a hand toward the entryway. "Come, Delores. Where is your sense of adventure?"

Delores took a deep breath. Their very atoms would intermingle? Infused with the power of slime? Her mind galloped past the fear. She had to make her move. This might be her only chance.

"Well," she said hesitantly. "I don't know. You never do know with highly experimental scientific equipment." She frowned at the entryway to the softly humming machine. "Sometimes—it can go wrong."

"You're right," Edward replied, his voice for the first time seeming to hold a seed of doubt. He, too, stared into the gadget-cluttered room. "Sometimes, with highly experimental scientific equipment, it almost seems it"—something caught in what might have been the monster's throat—"it *has* to go wrong."

"Could it be a Law of the Cineverse?" Delores asked innocently.

"Let us hope not," Edward answered, but he offered no other explanation. The humming sound appeared to grow louder from the room beyond, as if the machine were impatient with their hesitation.

This was it, then. She looked straight into those two tiny red glowing things that could have been Edward's eyes. "Perhaps—if you went in there first."

"I suppose," Edward replied grimly, "it is my duty."

He took a step inside the room. Now, the humming really did increase, both in pitch and volume. Edward took another step, and the hum again responded by shifting to an even higher level.

It had to be now, while what might have been his back was turned.

"Sorry, Edward!" Delores called softly as she bolted across the hall for the opposite door. Edward mumbled something behind her, lost in the ever-increasing hum.

She only had to run a few feet, but with each step she imagined Edward's mushy hand on her shoulder. She reached the entryway to the EXPERIMENTAL ANIMAL LAB. The Slime Monster hadn't missed her yet. Fortunately for her, the door was unlocked. She ran into the lab and slammed the door behind her.

Even with the door closed, she could hear the anguished roar of the Slime Monster. Edward had discovered she was gone.

And the Slime Monster's roar was answered from within the lab, from every animal in every cage—a great caterwauling cacophony that mixed barks and bleats, crows and coos, roars and rabbit cries. She had never heard so intense a sound. If Edward had any doubt about where Delores had disappeared, he surely knew now.

She forced herself to calm down, and examine the room she now found herself in. It was very bright, lit by brilliant Southern California sunshine pouring in through the floor-to-ceiling windows. She wondered if it ever rained on this advanced scientific world. She pushed the inappropriate thought from her head, and concentrated on the large room, with row after row of shining steel cages surrounded by tables, chairs, desks, walls—all antiseptic white. She had to find somewhere to hide—but where, in this ordered, bright existence?

She walked down the nearest row of cages, ready to look away if she saw a rabbit or chimpanzee plugged full of tubes in the name of science. Actually, however, the animal occupants—rabbits and white rats mostly, but also the occasional chicken and chimpanzee—seemed relatively well-fed and unmolested.

Delores should have remembered this from Hero School. The most they ever did in terms of "experimentation" on most movie worlds, especially bright, Southern California movie worlds, was to have chimps learn sign language and rats run mazes. Well, actually, this being an Institute of Very Advanced Science, she imagined the animals occasionally got injected with an invisibility formula or transported to the fourth dimension—but nothing that would actually hurt the creatures. They didn't do the really dangerous experiments on animals on this kind of movie world. From what she recalled from her courses in movie history, they were much more likely to perform those kind of experiments on humans.

The largest of all the cages, perhaps eight feet high and ten feet long, was empty. Delores frowned down at a neatly lettered sign.

ORANGUTANG it read. OOGIE. Perhaps, she thought, the missing animal was somewhere practicing sign language at this very minute.

She heard the door to the lab open as she reached the far end of the row. She flattened herself against the side of the farthest cage.

"Delores?" Edward's unmistakable voice called. "Come, my bride-to-be. It does no good to postpone the inevitable."

There were no doors in the far wall of the room; no exit whatsoever at this end of the lab. Edward would surely spot her if she tried to cross the lab to the door. She might be able to open one of those floor-to-ceiling windows a dozen feet to her right, if she could reach them without Edward seeing her. And even then, the windows looked out over treetops. How high above ground level would this lab be? The picturesque wooden frames would surely make a noise when opened, and what if there was then no way to get down from this upper story of the Institute?

Delores had nowhere to go. This place was an antiseptic trap.

Perhaps, if she couldn't find a hiding place, she could come up with a diversion. She glanced quickly around this end of the lab. There wasn't much here except for a moderate-sized panel, maybe three feet by four, built into the far wall; a gleaming metal collection of switches, buttons, and dials bearing a neatly lettered sign: CONTROL CENTER.

Did this movie-poster-sized metal board control all of the experiments in the animal lab? She stepped closer so that she could more carefully read the smaller, though no less neatly hand-lettered, signs that were posted above each of the controls. One sign in particular caught her attention—the one above the large red lever—the one marked: UNIVERSAL CAGE RELEASE.

Maybe, Delores thought, this would provide the very diversion she needed.

But where was Edward? Someone whose feet were composed of slime didn't make a great deal of noise.

"There is no escape," intoned Edward's voice, much closer than before. "Time to transmogrify."

The Slime Monster was almost on top of her! Delores had to do something fast!

She pulled the red lever.

There was another great noise, fully the equal of the

animals' earlier roar, although this time it was the sound of metal against metal, as locks popped open, hinges groaned, and bars screeched aside.

All sorts of creatures erupted from their cages. Twenty-foot-long snakes slithered past foot-long cockroaches. Barking dogs chased yowling cats. The chimps cavorted around the rabbits, rats, and chickens. There were lizards and frogs in here, too, hopping and scurrying every which way. Delores also thought she heard the squealing of pigs, the baahing of sheep, and the mooing of cows from the far side of the lab.

This was an even better diversion than Delores had originally imagined. She turned toward the window.

There was a slime monster standing in her path.

"There is no getting away," Edward murmured. "It is destiny."

Not now, when she was so close. Not now, when there were all these animals. Delores tried to pivot away, and almost fell. She couldn't move! Well, actually, she could move as much as she wanted, more than she wanted, actually, although that movement consisted largely of slipping and sliding. She looked down. It was no wonder she couldn't get any traction. The floor around her feet was coated with a good three inches of slime.

"Sorry about your shoes," Edward apologized. "But look on the bright side. After transmogrification, you probably will never need shoes again."

He reached over and grabbed her with an exceedingly long arm. He lifted her out of the muck and carried her, without effort, out of the lab and across the hall to the waiting machine.

The machine hummed in greeting.

Edward stepped inside, Delores still in tow. The red lights blinked rhythmically. The machine's hum surrounded them, high, loud, and happy—a hum of welcome, and perhaps a hum of triumph.

She was to be transmogrified.

Delores tried to fight her captivity, to somehow free herself from the monster's grip. But Edward's hold on her was strong and sure, and every time she tried to get her own grip on some part of the monster's anatomy, her hands sank into the muck.

"Resistance is useless," Edward remarked casually. "As long as there's water around, we monsters can make ourselves slimy or solid at will." He plunked Delores down in the chair on the left. "It's very handy around the house," he added as he strapped her arms tight against her body, then tied the chair's leather thong behind Delores' back.

"Poor Delores," Edward said as he shambled toward the opposite seat. "You have to change with the times." He sat, and pushed a large green button labeled START on the middle of the console before him. "After this, we shall truly be made for each other."

The humming became even louder and more insistent, the red lights flashing even more rapidly than before, as if the machine were getting really excited. Words flashed across a video monitor directly before Delores.

TRANSMOGRIFICATION SEQUENCE COMMENCING.

Those words were wiped away by a new sentence:

STRAP SUBJECT IN SEAT A.

Edward nodded pleasantly. "Subject. That's you."

STRAP YOURSELF IN SEAT B appeared on the video monitor.

"Of course." The Slime Monster found two halves of a seat belt to either side of his seat and buckled himself in. "And now?"

PRESS ANY KEY WHEN READY the machine informed them.

Edward punched something at random.

IF YOU WANT TO TRANSMOGRIFY, the machine responded, PRESS Y.

The Slime Monster did as he was instructed.

ARE YOU SURE?

Edward pressed YES a second time.

Delores heard another noise above the hum, a buzzing of some sort.

What might have been Edward's mouth seemed to frown. "Is there a fly in here?"

TRANSMOGRIFICATION CYCLE COMMENCED, was the machine's message.

"We can't have a fly in here!" Edward yelled in real panic. "Its atoms could intermingle with ours, causing who knows what damage!"

IF FOR ANY REASON, the machine's video monitor began. . . .

There was something else in here besides the fly. Something that was hopping.

"Toads?" Edward shouted. "How did toads—"

But there were more than toads hopping. Edward stared at the white, fluffy, bouncing things, in what might have been a look of horror.

"Bunnies?" he asked, his voice barely a whisper.

. . . YOU WISH TO TERMINATE CYCLE— the machine continued calmly.

Something barked.

"Dogs?" Edward's voice rose again towards hysteria.

Something else clucked.

"Chickens?" With that single word, the monster's voice reached that hysteria, and perhaps a bit more.

Delores realized that Edward had left the door open, and the animals, freed of their cages, had found them.

—PRESS ESCAPE BEFORE CHIME, the video monitor finished helpfully.

Edward nodded all too rapidly to Delores. "You were right."

Hop, went the toads. Hop, hop hop.

"I was a fool," the monster admitted.

Bzzz, went the flying insects. *Bzzz, bzzz, bzzz*.

"Neither man nor monster was meant to tamper with forces like this!"

Bounce, went the bunnies. Bounce bounce bounce.

"But all is not lost," Edward continued.

Bark, went the dogs. *Bark, bark, bark*. The room was filled with a dozen other animal noises from cries to coos, baahs to bleats.

The Slime Monster turned back to study the console. "All

I have to do is turn it off before the warning chime."

The humming and all other noise in the room ceased, and the sudden silence was filled with a clear, bell-like tone.

The warning chime had come and gone.

Cluck, went the chickens. *Cluck, cluck, cluck*.

The hum returned, so loud and high now it was almost a shriek, as both Delores and Edward—and all the animals around them—were bathed in pure, white light.

Edward screamed, a sound that now seemed more animal than slime. Delores closed her eyes. The whole room was vibrating, and more—she was vibrating. She was being transmogrified—infused with bits and pieces of all the things that occupied this room. What if the wrong bits ended up in the wrong places? It felt as if somebody were scrambling her for an omelet.

Edward screamed again. The other creatures in here weren't being silent either, although their cries were unlike anything Delores had ever heard.

The humming cut off abruptly. The blinding light disappeared.

But something in Delores had changed—if she could still be called Delores.

Would she ever see Roger again?

And then it got really dark. She couldn't see anything.

Maybe, Delores thought, she no longer had anything to see with.

8

Everyone stared at the tank.

The thing roared more like an enraged beast than a machine, underscored by the percussive clank of the heavy metal treads tearing up the asphalt. The ground quaked as the armored engine of death approached. The air was full of dust, and the tang of machine oil.

The tank was headed straight for them, slowly, relentlessly. But no one moved. The rest of Roger's companions appeared to be frozen in fear.

In a way, Roger couldn't blame the others. The tank seemed all wrong for this time and place, as if the Cop Movie world had suddenly veered into a desert war film. But then, Roger supposed, that was the Change.

The tank's gun turret swiveled and jerked, shooting out a projectile, followed by a lance of flame. They were being fired on! Roger took a step away.

No one else moved.

The shell sailed over their heads. It hadn't been aimed at them after all. Professor Peril was aiming for dramatic effect—and the thick steel pole that supported the rusted train tracks overhead.

The shell hit the base of the pole, exploding in a great cloud of dust.

Still, no one moved, their faces beaten by the squalling dirt. Perhaps, Roger realized, they *couldn't* move—there was something so wrong about the tank being here that it prevented them from moving, as if the Change was so profound that it locked their mental gears in place. Only Roger, with his non-Cineverse mind, was free of the paradox's grip.

If this was the sort of thing the Change brought, it was far worse than Roger had imagined.

Still the tank ground forward. The exploding dust cleared, and the steel pole and the rusted tracks above were no longer there.

Roger looked back at his fellows, all unnaturally immobile, five statues staring at their imminent destruction.

The tank stopped, its roaring engine shifting to a whispering idle, causing Roger to turn and stare with all the others.

The hatch popped open on the top of the tank turret. A steel-helmeted Professor Peril smiled malevolently.

"Not enough, heh?" He pointed one precise finger at the crowd standing before him. "Very well. I'm going to economically run over all of you!"

Peril's brief, to-the-point diabolical laughter was lost in the roar as the tank ground forward once more.

"Guys!" Roger called. "It's time to get out of here!"

There was still no response.

No, wait. Roger saw Big Louie twitch, his face screwed up in pain, as if any movement at all on his part required a supreme effort of will.

"Roger!" the sidekick's sidekick managed between clenched teeth. "You gotta say something!"

Roger frowned. Hadn't he already said something, any number of things, really, to his totally unresponsive audience? Even Big Louie had once again become as still as the others, although Roger thought there might be a new, pleading look in the sidekick's eyes.

Wait a moment. Unresponsive audience? Like a *movie theatre audience*?

Roger had to remember he had a new role in the Cineverse. He had spoken, yes, but only as Roger Gordon, average guy. From here on in, whenever he faced danger, whether from suspicious officers of the law or a marauding metal engine of destruction, he had to speak as Captain Crusader.

It wasn't all that easy to think of aphorisms when there

was a tank bearing down on you. But Roger—or rather, Captain Crusader—had to do his best.

"Running is good for you!" he shouted over the grinding roar.

Did any of his friends move? It was hard to tell, but Roger thought he detected a twitch here, a spasm there. His theory, then, was correct, but Roger was going to have to be a bit more creative. Perhaps if he could find something with a touch more eloquence.

It was even harder to be eloquent when you had a tank bearing down on you. Roger shouted the first thing that came into his mind:

"He who hesitates is squashed!"

Even as the words left his mouth, Roger realized that they were far too derivative—so derivative, in fact, that Roger seemed to have made the situation worse. Whatever freedom, along with all twitches and spasms, his first comment had given his fellows had vanished, and all were frozen stiff before the tank's inexorable—and ever closer—approach.

This was it, then: Roger's last chance. Whatever discipline he had learned in public relations, he needed it now. There was a certain rhythm to a classic Captain Crusader caption, a rhythm Roger had to reproduce, while at the same time describing some essential truth that would not seem out of place in a seventh-grade social studies class.

The words flashed into his mind in a complete sentence, almost as if he were reading from a script. And this time, the words sounded right.

He spoke in a loud, clear voice:

"Jogging is the cardiovascularly correct way to see the world."

All of Roger's friends shook themselves, as if waking from a long sleep. And all of them ran out of the path of the rampaging tank as it rumbled past.

"Saints alive, Captain Crusader," Officer O'Clanrahan cheered. "I knew you wouldn't let us down!"

"A complete thought is a happy thought," Roger agreed,

the words tumbling from his tongue without conscious effort. The aphorism came so quickly, in fact, it was a little frightening. Becoming Captain Crusader was more than a great responsibility, Roger realized—a life as the hero's hero might mean some fundamental changes in how he viewed the world, and even in his own self-image.

Roger's thoughts were interrupted by a warning blast of horns and tympani. Dwight started to bark.

"Oh, no!" Big Louie warned. "Peril's turned the tank around. He's coming for us again!"

Roger turned around to see the truth in Louie's summary—the tank was rumbling toward them once more. Professor Peril shook his fist at them from the open turret.

This time, at least, no one was frozen. Not that there was any direction to their movement. In fact, Roger's followers seemed to be running in all directions at once. But at least they were running. Despite whatever discrepancy threatened the fabric of the Cineverse, Roger's—or rather, Captain Crusader's—corrective aphorism seemed to have shifted the balance on this particular movie world so that all his company could act.

Wow. *Whatever discrepancy threatened the fabric of the Cineverse?* Roger realized he was even beginning to think like Captain Crusader.

Somehow, though, Captain Crusader had to stop this tank. The music, suddenly back in full force, was building to a fever pitch. Roger still didn't know where that orchestra originated, but he knew what that music meant, with its blaring horns and beating drums. They were coming to the Big Action Scene.

"Bark, bark, yip arf!" the Wonder Dog remarked.

"Dwight suggests that we come up with some counter-strategy," Big Louie translated.

"I think one well-placed shot with a six-shooter should fix Peril once and for all," Doc drawled. He glanced at Roger. "Six-shooters will work in these here parts, won't they?"

Roger reassured Doc, that, as long as other guns—not

to mention tanks—worked on this particular movie world, six-shooters should fit perfectly with the local version of movie magic.

"Spoken like Captain Crusader!" Louie shouted encouragingly.

"Tarnation!" Doc cursed, easing his palm from the gun hammer. "I can't get a clear shot."

Roger saw Doc's problem. The tank was once again surrounded by an opaque cloud of dust.

"Cloud of dust not stop Zabana!" The well-muscled Prince of the Jungle stepped forward. "Zabana use his jungle-bred reflexes and jump on tank like he jump on fear-maddened elephant!"

He flexed his well-muscled forehead.

"First Zabana judge how fast elephant is coming."

Zabana hunkered down into his famous jungle crouch.

"Then jungle prince set himself to spring." He smiled with the confidence of one who was truly ruler of the jungle.

"Now Zabana use language of animals to distract fear-maddened—" Zabana hesitated, the smile vanished from his face. "How you call fear-maddened tank?"

The dust around the tank cleared enough for Roger to see the gun barrel swivel towards them.

"I have a better idea," he interjected. "Let's get out of here!"

This time, the others agreed, and followed Roger in a full-scale retreat.

"Beggin' your pardon," Officer O'Clanrahan remarked as he puffed by Roger's side. "Retreating may be advisable, but is it truly a Captain Crusader thing to do?"

Oh, dear. Roger hadn't thought of that. If his actions were inappropriate, would it affect his standing as the hero's hero?

But what other action could he take? Roger knew now that Captain Crusader sayings worked on people in the Cineverse. But would they work on machines?

If he could stop the tank in its tracks—what a heroic action that would be! And if they captured Professor Peril, perhaps they could even learn the whereabouts of Doctor Dread so that they could bring this Change under control. Even if Peril wouldn't speak, perhaps Dwight could pick up Dread's scent from the Professor and lead them to the archfiend's hideout, in the same way the Wonder Dog had helped Delores find Captain Crusader.

Delores. The name of the woman of his dreams caused Roger's heart to skip a beat. But how could he find Delores while he was battling the Change with his every breath? No, Roger knew, he had to halt the Change first if he and Delores were going to have any chance at happiness.

And that meant stopping the onrushing tank—somehow.

Roger stopped as the others ran on.

He turned to face his adversary. Uncounted tons of metal malice bore down upon him.

Roger realized he had another problem, not all that different from Zabana's recent dilemma. What did you say—what did even Captain Crusader say—to a tank? Or perhaps you didn't speak to the tank, but to the person inside. In that case—what did you say to Professor Peril?

There was only one way to find out.

"A tank a day keeps your problems away," Roger shouted over the armored machine's never-ending roar.

The tank kept on coming. And no wonder, Roger thought. What a lackluster first effort! That aphorism had had none of the rhythm, none of the élan, of the proper Captain Crusader quote.

He'd have to try harder, or he'd be run over in a matter of seconds. He drew on whatever inner resources he still possessed, combined with his ever-growing appreciation of tank treads. Yes! He thought he had it this time.

Roger screamed with every ounce of energy in his soul:

"A modern combat vehicle means never having to say you're sorry."

All his company stopped their flight to turn and applaud. Roger sighed happily. That had been a good one.

But the tank kept on coming.

Maybe, Roger considered, when you were driving a tank,

you couldn't hear any Captain Crusader sayings.

He turned and ran with redoubled speed. His companions joined him.

"Bark, bark! Yip, yip!"

"Dwight smells the harbor," Big Louie helpfully translated.

The harbor? What was the Wonder Dog trying to tell them? Now that Dwight mentioned it, Roger did smell a salt tang mixed with the odor of burning machine oil. But what did this mean?

Roger had a cold chill of recognition as he remembered his movies.

There was an even better way to end a car chase than smashing into trash cans.

They had reached the end of one of the extremely long warehouses. With barely a second's hesitation, Roger turned right and headed downhill.

"Yip, yip!" the Wonder Dog called from behind. "Bark, bark!"

"Wait a minute!" Big Louie interjected. "Dwight says that way only leads to the docks!"

"Exactly!" Roger shouted triumphantly. "Follow me, everybody!"

Roger and the others rushed down the sloping street, with the tank in close pursuit. It was only two short blocks to an old fisherman's pier.

Roger waited until they were scant feet away from the weathered wood.

"Okay, everybody!" he yelled as he veered to his right. "Away from the dock! Scatter!"

Everyone on foot turned quickly.

The tank was not so agile. It plowed straight ahead, out onto the aged wooden pilings—pilings that, even when new, were not meant to take the weight of a death-dealing mass of sinister steel.

There was a great roar and a rending of wood as the tank slid into the water, taking half the dock with it.

"Curse you, Captain Crusader!" Professor Peril shook

his fist at them from his station at the falling tank turret.

The tank hit the water and sank quickly.

"Bark arf!" Dwight announced. "Yip bark!"

"Dwight says we can't let Peril drown," Louie interpreted. "That's not the hero's way!"

It was worse than that, Roger realized. If they lost Professor Peril, they lost their link to Doctor Dread, and the heart of the Change. Without that link, they might never be able to save the Cineverse—and Roger might never see Delores again!

It was time for more than words. It was time for action. And Roger should have no trouble with a straightforward hero-rescue situation like this. Now that the tank was quiet, his Captain Crusader sayings could get him out of any danger—couldn't they?

Roger and Dwight the Wonder Dog simultaneously dove into the drink.

The water was so cold that it took Roger's breath away. And the water was moving, too. The tank was sinking so fast that it had formed a whirlpool at the surface, sucking everything else down behind it—everything, including Roger and Dwight.

The vortex closed overhead, and they were underwater, going down fast.

Roger realized then that he had neglected to consider one eventuality. You couldn't spout clever sayings—you couldn't say anything—if your mouth was full of water.

Apparently, even Captain Crusader could drown.

9

"Roger?" Big Louie called down into the still water at the end of the dock. All was quiet—far too quiet.

A moment before, Roger had used his knowledge of movie worlds, combined with his newfound leadership as Captain Crusader, to lure Professor Peril and his tank into the murky waters at the end of the pier. But Louie realized now that Roger, as the hero's hero, could not let even someone as nefarious as Peril drown. Roger had immediately jumped in the water as well, followed quickly by the almost-as-heroic Dwight the Wonder Dog. Both of them went down beneath the churning waves. But neither they, nor Professor Peril, had surfaced again.

"Mother of mercy!" For a change, Officer O'Clanrahan said what Louie was thinking. "They're gone? Dwight the Wonder Dog is gone?"

"No!" Louie objected. "Wait a minute!" O'Clanrahan was suggesting that Dwight and Roger and Peril were all beyond hope, sucked away by treacherous currents and drowned beneath the incoming tide. Louie couldn't accept it; this sort of thing went against everything a sidekick stood for. Maybe Roger Gordon could fall victim to such a fate, but not the hero's hero—not Captain Crusader!

"Roger!" Louie called, but the only answer was the soft lap of the waves against the pilings beneath the dock.

Perhaps it was only his sidekick nature, but Louie still wasn't ready to give up. Maybe he was doing something wrong—like, Louie realized, calling the wrong individual.

Maybe, just maybe, he had to address the hero's hero by name.

"Captain Crusader?" Louie yelled.

But the only answer was the gentle shushing of the sea wind and the distant sound of a lone, clanging buoy.

"We might as well face it, boyos," Officer O'Clanrahan ventured with a sigh. "They're gone to the briny deep." He turned and took a step toward shore.

"Tarnation!" Doc yelled, pointing to a spot not three feet from O'Clanrahan's boots. "Look what's washed up against the dock!"

Louie knelt down to get a better look. There, pushed against the piling by the never-ending waves, were a book, *The Cineverse From A to Zed*—and a small, round, gray, incredibly cheaply made, piece of plastic.

Louie pulled both from the water. "It's Roger's guidebook—and his Captain Crusader Decoder Ring!"

Zabana frowned down at the objects in Louie's hands. "What this mean?"

Louie could take no joy in his discoveries. There could be no denying it now. It was one of the true signs of the Cineverse—once you found someone's Decoder Ring, it meant, well—

"It means Roger is gone," Louie replied softly.

"Roger gone?" Zabana demanded. "That impossible!"

"It is durned peculiar," Doc agreed. "He jumps in the drink and disappears, just like that? I never seen its like in all my years as a merchant seaman."

"Zabana not accept this!" the jungle prince announced. "We find out what really happen. Zabana call fish!"

Zabana paused a moment in thought. "Ah! Jungle prince remember!" He cupped his hands to his mouth and shouted down to the water. "Gurgle gurgle greech caroo!"

He stared at the murky waves expectantly, but the only answer was the distant cry of a pair of gulls, and the roar of an automobile as it raced onto the dock.

The beat-up yellow Chevy screeched to a halt a few feet away as Zabana looked up in consternation. The cops got out, slamming the doors behind them.

"No fish?" Zabana bemoaned to no one in particular.

"You don't expect any fish in *this* harbor, do you?" Three-day-growth asked sarcastically.

"Unless there was one in a trash bag—" Earring ventured.

"Yeah, or maybe stuck with a syringe," Three-day-growth concluded. He pointed to Big Louie. "So what happened here?"

Louie summarized the recent events in his best sidekick manner.

Three-day-growth grunted when he was through. "It's the treacherous tides around here—especially around the full moon."

"Yeah," Earring added as he nodded toward the horizon, "and the wicked undertow from the ocean out there—"

"Not to mention all those cross currents caused by the irresponsible use of pleasure vehicles," Three-day-growth finished. "Well, Peril's case is closed. It looks like our job is finished here."

"Finished?" Zabana demanded. "How can be finished when Captain Crusader underwater?"

"Sorry." Earring shrugged. "No longer our jurisdiction."

Louie felt a cold chill at the nape of his short but sturdy neck—a chill that could freeze his entire form. Not the cops' jurisdiction? This, along with Roger's sudden disappearance, sounded more and more like the Change!

But Zabana was more direct in his displeasure. He took a threatening step in the policemen's direction.

"Faith and begorrah!" Officer O'Clanrahan protested. "The coppers are only doin' their job!"

Only doing their job? Louie thought. O'Clanrahan must have been more shaken by the loss of the Wonder Dog than even Louie imagined.

"Still haven't lost the brogue, huh?" Earring remarked.

O'Clanrahan took a startled step backward.

"And still wearing that loincloth, I see," Earring addressed Zabana in a less than approving tone.

Zabana made a sound deep in his throat that betrayed his jungle origins.

Louie frowned. He could see this confrontation escalating into another real conflict situation, exactly like their first encounter with these two—and this time, there was no Captain Crusader to come up with a pithy saying to diffuse the tension and make things right.

The two cops looked at each other and reached for their guns.

"No!" Big Louie shouted. The two cops stopped and stared. He stepped forward, standing as tall as he was able. Without Captain Crusader here, it was up to him.

"Remember what happened the last time you saw us?" Louie asked quickly. "We were—all of us—ready to fight without thinking. That is, we were until Captain Crusader stepped forward and stirred us with his deeply meaningful words—words that brought us back to our senses, and led us to understand and appreciate each other."

Louie's voice rose as he choked back the emotion building inside him. "Now, though, Captain Crusader has vanished. Perhaps, he is even dead. But the spirit of Captain Crusader cannot die! And it is that spirit we must remember; that spirit that must bring us back to our senses once again!"

The cops looked at each other and put away their guns.

"I'd say our job is just about finished here," Three-day-growth admitted.

"Yeah," Earring agreed. "No reason to bother these nice folks."

The two cops got back in their battered Chevy, and the car roared off the dock in reverse.

"Tarnation!" Doc exclaimed. "That was pretty good speechifyin'. But do you have the faintest idee what we should do next?"

"Zabana dive in water!" the jungle prince volunteered. "Search for Roger!"

But Louie placed a restraining hand against one of Zabana's bulging thews. "No, Zabana. You heard what the cops said. We've already lost Captain Crusader. I don't want to lose you as well. We need all our strength for the fight ahead.''

He turned to Doc. ''Oddly enough, I do have an idea of what we should do. Remember, I used to be a member of Dread's gang. I know all his major hideouts—it's only a matter of time before we stumble on the one he's using now.'' He paused to look at his three fellows. ''But when we do, we must be prepared. We must have the proper weapon.''

He held up the soggy copy of *The Cineverse From A to Zed*.

''Book is weapon?'' Zabana asked, still apparently confounded by Louie's newfound forcefulness.

''Well, no,'' Louie admitted, ''but it can lead us to a weapon.''

Officer O'Clanrahan still seemed unconvinced. ''Faith and begorrah! How can any weapon match the might of Dread?''

''I don't intend to use conventional weapons,'' Louie replied. ''It's time for psychological warfare. It's time for''—he paused in a manner that would have done Dread proud—''bunnies.''

''Bunnies!'' Zabana exclaimed in sudden comprehension. ''Dread putty in hands of bunnies. But how we get Dread back to bunny world?''

''That would seem to be our biggest problem,'' Louie agreed with a nod. Doctor Dread was indeed putty in the bunnies' paws, his entire personality changing amidst the animated rabbits, much the same way noted scientist Dr. Dee Dee Davenport had been transformed into a beach bunny when confronted by endless expanses of sand and three-chord surf guitar. It was something that happened to some people in the Cineverse, when they discovered a world that somehow fit their personalities all too well.

Still, because of the possibility of this personality shift, Dread was all too wary of animated worlds. There seemed, therefore, as Zabana had pointed out, to be no direct method to get Dread to the bunnies. But Louie knew more than direct methods. On the *Film Noir* world that was his home, deviousness was a way of life.

"But there is another way," he continued. "If we can't bring Dread to the bunnies, we'll bring the bunnies to Dread!"

"Whoo-eee!" Doc whooped enthusiastically. "Now *that's* a plan!"

"Now," Louie remarked as he tucked the Captain Crusader Ring into the pocket of his double-breasted blazer, "if I can keep the pages of this thing from sticking together, maybe I can locate our first destination. Ah! Here it is, in the index, under 'Bunnies, fluffy.' " He looked up at the others. "Well, gather round, fellas. We've got a Cineverse to save!"

The three other men all grabbed a piece of Louie's coat as he pulled out the ring and twisted.

"See you in the funny papers!"

They heard the sound of galloping horses through the blue smoke.

"Cartoon horses, no doubt," Louie reassured the others. "Cartoon horses and cartoon bunnies would go very well together."

Then they heard the sound of grunts and shouts amid the pounding hooves.

"Sound like cartoon horses exercising?" Zabana asked tentatively.

But the next sound seemed even more out of place—the clash of metal against metal.

"Tarnation!" Doc exclaimed. "I know that sound from my years as a world-class duelist. That's a sword fight!"

Louie frowned. Whatever it was, it sure didn't sound like bunnies.

"Mother of mercy!" Officer O'Clanrahan announced as the smoke cleared. "I knew this was going to be a bad idea."

Louie stared at the suddenly revealed countryside. He didn't know whether it was bad or not, but it was certainly wrong. They had materialized, not in the middle of an animated cartoon, but on a dusty plain, complete with large boulders and the occasional scrubby tree. And on this plain were half a dozen men, dressed only in sandals and short, skirt-like loincloths that covered them only from the waist to the upper thigh, six very well-muscled men who fought, three against three, with gleaming broadswords.

The men in sandals had noticed them as well, the three in light loincloths quickly dispatching the three in darker costumes, with a series of quick but none-too-convincing sword strokes. The three survivors turned menacingly toward Louie and his fellows.

"Intruders!" a woman's voice called from beyond the battle. "Who now dares confront Hippolita, Oracle of Venus?"

A chariot pulled by a pair of snow-white horses emerged from between a pair of boulders. The musclemen stepped aside to allow the chariot to thunder forward, turning sharply as it stopped.

"All hail Hippolita!" the three musclemen chanted.

A tall woman stepped from the chariot to confront Louie and the others. She was wearing a white robe cut so that it revealed one of her shapely shoulders and most of her shapely legs. Her face was framed by long blond hair, and too much eye makeup.

"Well," she demanded imperiously. "Why don't you answer me?"

"Uh—" Louie replied, temporarily taken aback. Wasn't there something wrong with the way her lips moved? Still, even if there was, Louie realized he'd better come up with an answer. "We are but humble travelers, seeking the truth."

"Sound like spies to me!" one of the musclemen interjected. Yes, Louie noticed, this fellow seemed to be having a similar problem with his mouth muscles, with too many syllables for the movement of his lips. What strange secret did this world hold to afflict its denizens so?

"They should know who they are facing," the muscleman barked. He pointed to his two fellows. "We are all noble warriors: The son of Samson, the nephew of Hercules, and the second cousin of Goliath."

"Second cousin?" Zabana asked doubtfully.

"On his mother's side, but still a blood relation!" the muscleman growled.

Louie thought it was only polite to introduce his company as well.

"Big Louie?" Hippolita asked. "Could that mean 'Born out of rock'?"

It really was somewhat disconcerting, the way the movement of her lips never quite matched the sound of her words. But Louie could not become mesmerized by this peculiarity.

"Not that I know of," he managed to reply. This wasn't going at all the way he had hoped. They should be talking with fluffy bunnies, not barbarians with broadswords. This was the problem with being a sidekick—if he was a hero, he'd probably already have come up with a way to get out of this place and on with their real business.

"What of your fellows?" the oracle continued in the same imperious tone. That was another thing, Louie realized—for an all-seeing sort of person, which was what the Oracle of Venus was, after all, she asked an awful lot of questions, didn't she? Then again, there were these three menacing guys with their swords. Louie continued his introductions.

"Doc?" Hippolita frowned. "Too short to mean 'Born out of rock'. Officer O'Clanrahan? It has possibilities."

The rotund policeman nodded uncertainly, not quite sure if he were being paid a compliment.

"Still," Hippolita continued doubtfully, "he doesn't quite seem like the 'Born out of rock' type."

"None of them look worthy of being 'Born out of rock'!" the son of Samson jeered. "I say we should put them to the sword!"

"Swords?" The Prince of the Jungle stepped forward. "Zabana laugh at swords!"

The nephew of Hercules shook his head in amazement. "This fellow could be the one!"

"He has definite 'Born out of rock' characteristics," Goliath's second-cousin-on-his-mother's-side agreed.

"And Zabana," the son of Samson mused. "It sounds right. Surely it must mean 'Born out of rock'!"

"Actually, it mean 'big, hairless orangutang,' " Zabana admitted.

"Close enough!" Hippolita declared. "The prophecy has come true!"

"All hail Hippolita!" the three musclemen chorused as they sheathed their swords.

The prophecy had come true? The swords had gone away? Louie whistled softly to himself. Did this mean they were saved?

"Our champion has come!" the son of Samson declared.

"The forces of right will triumph!" the nephew of Hercules joined in.

"Finally," the second-cousin-on-his-mother's-side of Goliath explained, "someone who will face the Pit of Absurdity!"

The Pit of Absurdity? That didn't sound like being saved to Big Louie. He still had the feeling that this sort of thing wouldn't be happening if they were being led by a full-fledged hero type.

The situation was so bad that even Zabana's jungle-bred brain noticed a certain discrepancy.

"Pit of Absurdity!" the jungle prince exclaimed. "Wait minute!"

"Oh, that's right," Hippolita murmured with the slightest of alluring smiles. "We have to decide what to do with your slaves. Would you like them to accompany you, or shall we kill them now?"

Slaves? Oh dear, Louie thought, this was getting completely out of hand. And it seemed that those three musclemen had drawn their swords again very enthusiastically.

"Uh—" Zabana stared, momentarily taken aback by having to make a choice. "Friends come with Zabana."

"Very well." Hippolita waved to her musclemen. "Bring them along."

Louie felt the point of a sword in his back as Hippolita led the way to the boulders. Louie followed, as did both Doc and Officer O'Clanrahan. Zabana sprang forward, his jungle muscles taut.

"When the troops of Romulus and Remus face the Spartans, we must have the Jewel of the Seven Cities to ensure our victory!" Hippolita explained. "That is why we have been waiting for our champion, to rescue the jewel from the terrors of the Pit!"

Louie didn't like this 'terrors of the pit' talk. It sounded a little like that time they had stumbled onto the home planet of the Slime Monster. Louie shivered despite himself. Now that he thought about it, he hadn't liked much of anything that had happened since they had landed on this particular movie world. There had to be another way—but of course there was! He simply had to get his fellow adventurers together again, and he could use the ring!

He felt in his jacket pocket. The ring wasn't there.

"Do you have any questions before we take you to the Pit of Absurdity?" Hippolita asked.

Zabana pondered this for a minute, then asked at last: "Where bunnies?"

The three musclemen exchanged knowing looks.

"Is there any doubt about the prophecy now?" the nephew of Hercules asked with a grin.

"He is a match for the Pit of Absurdity!" The son of Samson nodded knowingly.

"This one is truly 'Born out of rock'!" the second cousin, and not by marriage, either, of Goliath rejoined.

Where could Louie have put the ring? A real hero wouldn't have lost the ring, would he? Now, now, he told himself, he had to calm down. It was surely still some distance to this pit. The ring had to be in one of his pockets. He'd find it in plenty of time.

Hippolita led them past the boulders. She pointed at a large hole in the ground in front of her. "And here, noble hero, is the Pit."

The Pit of Absurdity was only around the next boulder?

What kind of low-budget movie world was this? How could he possibly find the ring now?

"Zabana laugh at Pit!" the jungle prince declared.

"So we hope," Hippolita replied.

But the musclemen weren't laughing. Louie felt the sword-point pushing him to the lip of the precipice.

"Into the Pit!" commanded the Oracle of Venus.

Zabana jumped as the three others were pushed. The result was the same.

All four of them were falling into utter darkness.

10

It took Roger a moment to realize he was breathing. And a second moment to realize he was no longer surrounded by water, but by blue smoke.

HEY ROGER!

a voice rang out of the blueness.

LONG TIME, NO SEE!

Roger realized, even before the angelic choir kicked in, that he was once again in the presence of the Plotmaster.

SO, WHAT BRINGS YOU ALL THE WAY UP HERE?

the Plotmaster asked jovially.

All the way up here? Roger thought. He didn't even know where he was. The only thing he actually knew about this place was that there were always these darn singing angels going on and on in the background, and Roger could always count on being talked to by an imposing figure in blue, backlit so you couldn't see him very well. And what *brought* Roger? How could he have even found a nebulous destination like this in the first place?

The Plotmaster chuckled as he took a puff on his blue-smoke cigar.

AH, BUT FIND ME YOU DID, BOOBALA!
YOU'D BE SURPRISED WHAT YOU CAN DO,
ONCE YOU'VE BECOME CAPTAIN CRUSADER.

Roger did it? But he didn't even use his ring! And he certainly didn't say "See you in the funny papers!"

The Plotmaster answered him brusquely:

FACE IT, ROGER.
ONCE YOU'RE CAPTAIN CRUSADER
YOU DON'T NEED A RING.
YOU HAVE "METHODS."
SO WHAT'S YOUR PROBLEM?

"Uh—" Roger began, and realized that was the first word he had spoken since he had gotten here, even though the two of them seemed to be having a full-fledged conversation. He did notice, though, that the blue smoke had dissipated sufficiently for Roger to make out that dimly backlit shape smoking a cigar in front of him.

This time, the Plotmaster sounded the slightest bit peeved:

OH, I KNOW I COULD LOOK IT UP IN THE SCRIPT!
BUT TALKING ABOUT IT IS JUST SO MUCH MORE
PERSONAL.

"All right," Roger replied, and tried to quickly summarize everything that had happened since the arrival of his mother on the Beach Party planet, including their unexplained arrival on the Cop Movie world, the fact that Roger was hearing all this dramatic music, and his progress with Captain Crusader sayings.

But, the last thing he remembered, he was drowning, along with Dwight and Professor Peril. What had happened to the others?

"Yip, bark, yip!" Dwight remarked cheerfully from somewhere nearby.

The Plotmaster's reply held a twinge of wonder:

SAY, ISN'T THAT DWIGHT THE WONDER DOG?

Everybody, Roger remembered, knew Dwight the Wonder Dog.

"Bark, arf, bark bark!" Dwight answered.

YES, I AM THE PLOTMASTER.

"Yip, bark, arf arf, woof!" the dog quickly countered. The backlit man with the blue-smoke cigar nodded sagely.

YES,
AND THE PHILOSOPHICAL IMPLICATIONS
ARE INDEED STAGGERING.

"You're the Plotmaster?" a small, somewhat more human voice spoke from behind Roger. Roger turned around to see the army-fatigue-clad Professor Peril, doing his best to look as inconspicuous as possible on the light blue, never-ending plane where the Plotmaster held court. Apparently, his tank had been left behind on the Cop Movie world.

"There really *is* a Plotmaster?" Peril added, looking none too comfortable.

But Roger didn't have time to think about Peril's comfort. The Plotmaster had asked Roger if he had any problems, and, especially in his new role as Captain Crusader, he had a responsibility to answer. Besides what was going on in the Cineverse with the Change and all, Roger could think of two very definite problems. The first had to do with Delores and the Slime Monster—

The Plotmaster cleared his throat.

DELORES?
LISTEN, TAKE IT FROM SOMEONE WHO KNOWS.
FORGET ABOUT DELORES.

Forget about Delores? Suddenly, Roger didn't feel the least bit like Captain Crusader. Questions warred with each other in his head:

Shouldn't somebody with the total control of the Plotmaster be able to prevent this sort of thing?

Now that the Change was upon them again, did that mean there were never, ever going to be any more happy endings?

And what could have happened to Delores that was that bad?

LET'S JUST SAY
IT ISN'T PRETTY.

"Uh—" Professor Peril interrupted, "Mr. Plotmaster, sir? I have to explain a few things. I haven't always been on my best behavior."

Roger couldn't concentrate on what Peril was saying. He felt as if he had been kicked in the stomach by an iron boot. Delores was the whole reason he had gotten involved in the Cineverse in the first place. Sure, there had been other women in his life—actually, quite a few other women—but Delores had been different. There had been a communication between them that had been, well, unearthly. And now, something had happened to her, beyond even the power of the Plotmaster.

"Listen those sixty-three bank jobs," Peril explained, "and those seventeen diamond heists—"

Roger wasn't going to give up, even now. For one thing, giving up wasn't the sort of thing Captain Crusader did. And, who knew, in a place as vast and varied as the Cineverse, maybe there was some hope for Delores that even the Plotmaster didn't know about. And, if not, if what had happened to Delores was beyond remedying, perhaps—once Roger had found her again—he could at least make her comfortable, or put her out of her misery, or something.

Roger sighed. His first question to the Plotmaster had gotten the worst answer imaginable. He didn't even want to ask about that other thing—

OH, YES.
THE OTHER THING.
YOU MEAN YOUR MOTHER, DON'T YOU?

The Plotmaster paused and sighed.

I FEEL A CERTAIN RESPONSIBILITY FOR YOUR MOTHER.
YOU HAVE TO UNDERSTAND, ROGER.
SOMETIMES THE SCRIPT CALLS FOR SOMETHING EVEN I MIGHT NOT LIKE.
YOU'VE GOTTA HAVE CONFLICT, AFTER ALL.

"—and those seven hundred and twelve mortgages I foreclosed . . ." Peril continued.

Roger felt a certain responsibility toward his mother, too. Still, there was something about the Plotmaster's response—

"That's why my mother got zapped by the Zeta Ray?" Roger asked incredulously. "Conflict?"

"—and those innumerable train robberies," Peril went on miserably, "and those high-speed motorboat chases . . ."

YEAH, CONFLICT.
AND A PRETTY GOOD ONE, TOO.

Well, Roger supposed, if you thought about it that way. It was good for the Cineverse, maybe. But what about the needs of Roger Gordon—or the needs of Captain Crusader? He glanced distractedly at the still-babbling Peril.

"—and then there were those six Latin American revolutions I helped to foment," the cut-rate villain lamented economically. "And of course those three times I tried to take over the world—"

But Peril's confessions began to fade as Roger realized for the first time that he might have lost both the woman he loved, and his mother, too. Talk about heartbreak—

DON'T TALK TO ME ABOUT HEARTBREAK.
HEY, I'M THE PLOTMASTER!

The backlit man shook his cigar at Roger as the angelic chorus rose in the background.

DON'T DESPAIR, ROGER.
IT'S NOT HOPELESS.
IT'S NEVER HOPELESS.
WELL, ONCE IN A WHILE, IN THOSE FILMS WITH SUBTITLES,
IT DOES GET PRETTY CLOSE TO HOPELESS, DOESN'T IT?
BUT HEY,
WE WON'T LET THE CHANGE GET THAT FAR HERE, WILL WE?
WHO'S IN CHARGE HERE, ANYWAY?

"It wasn't my fault!" Peril wailed. "I was a victim of society!"

Roger didn't find anything the Plotmaster said the least bit reassuring. Instead, he felt a deep emptiness.

"But"—he began. He hesitated when he realized that the Plotmaster was still waiting for an answer to his question.

OH.

The Plotmaster answered himself:

I SUPPOSE I AM.

Yes, the Plotmaster was in charge, at least as far as Roger understood the setup around here. Still, Roger couldn't help it. He had to ask the next question:

"But can't you do *something*?"

"Well, I've confessed," Professor Peril demanded. "Aren't you going to say anything?"

But the Plotmaster had to answer Roger first. And, when he did answer, his voice was sadder than Roger had ever heard before, supported by the mournful dirge of the angelic choir, as if all of them were weighted down by a thousand plots gone wrong:

ALAS, THERE'S A DIFFERENCE, BOOBALA, BETWEEN BEING IN CHARGE AND BEING IN CONTROL.

The angelic choir shifted up an octave, and then another.

THAT'S WHY WE NEED CAPTAIN CRUSADER.
THAT'S WHY WE NEED YOU, ROGER.
IT'S UP TO YOU NOW.
GIVE 'EM ONE FOR THE PLOTMASTER!

"No!" the Professor interjected. "Ignore me, will you? Well, you do so at your own peril!"

Dwight barked as an ominously fizzing globe rolled to a stop mere inches from the Plotmaster's feet!

OH, NO!

The Plotmaster reacted in horror.

NOT A SMOKE BOMB!

"And not just any smoke bomb," replied the evil professor, barely able to keep his fiendish glee under control. "No, you are confronted by a genuine Professor Peril Smoke Bomb Economy Special—more bomb for your buck—accept no substitutions!" His announcement complete, the villain allowed his maniacal laughter to overwhelm him at last, as the immediate vicinity was filled with thick, black smoke.

"Bark, arf, yip!" Dwight announced.

COUGH!

the Plotmaster replied.

COUGH! COUGH! COUGH!

Roger was close to panic. Shouldn't Captain Crusader be doing something here?

"Ha!" the Professor announced abruptly. "My current triumph will be as nothing to our final victory, when I lead the forces of Doctor Dread back here to overwhelm the Plotmaster!"

Roger panicked at last. Could Peril do something like that? He supposed, with the Change, that anything was possible. Still, he couldn't help but think, in bringing Professor Peril here, had he—Roger Gordon—doomed the Plotmaster?

The Professor's laughter was cut off abruptly as Peril disappeared, beyond the reach of even Captain Crusader.

11

Mother Antoinette surveyed her new suite of rooms. Doctor Dread had tried, on very short notice, to liven up the dreary, barracks-like quality of the living quarters, importing a couple of wall-hangings from the Great Hall to cover the drab, gray walls. She especially liked the tapestry that depicted Lucretia Borgia poisoning her relatives—now, there was a woman with style. There were other festive touches in this place as well, like the ornate grillwork of the bars on the windows, and, of course, the decorative Iron Maiden. Part of her thought it was quite sweet of Dread to go to all this trouble, but the other, greater part of her knew this suite was only what she deserved.

She had been given one whole wing of the top floor of Dread's citadel. The doctor assured her that the occupant of the main room had been away for so long that he certainly wouldn't need it anymore, and the half-dozen guards and lackeys that had been displaced from the smaller rooms by this new arrangement did not feel inconvenienced in the least. Not that Mother Antoinette would have cared. Actually, now that she thought of it, she would like to inconvenience people on occasion—as many people as possible.

There was a knock on the door.

She strode quickly across the huge bedroom, her heels tapping a smart, martial beat atop the cold marble floor.

"Who's there?" she demanded.

"Antoinette!" a voice quavered on the other side of the thick oak door. "It's your Mengy!"

She smiled softly to herself as her fingers caressed the handle of her whip. Now that she had a place of her own, it was high time she and "her Mengy" spent some time alone. She opened the door.

Menge looked up at her and swallowed. "An—An—Antoinette."

"Why don't you come in and"—she raised one eyebrow and paused in that way they had around here—"get comfortable?"

Menge cleared his throat. "Most assuredly." He scurried into the room as Mother Antoinette slammed the door behind him. He stopped dead when he saw the very large bed with the black leather bedspread.

"My, this is quite—something." His gaze flicked about the room, resting briefly on the tapestries that covered the closets to either side, and a bit longer on the large night table covered with those various instruments Mother Antoinette thought might prove instructive—but his eyes returned, again and again, to the room's dominant piece of furniture.

"My," he said at last, "that's a—bed, isn't it?"

She smiled slightly. "This is my boudoir."

"Indeed it is." Mengy cleared his throat again. She wondered if he might be catching cold. "Perhaps, though, we could go somewhere else to—talk?"

There was an edge to Mother Antoinette's reply. "I believe this is the proper room—for everything."

"Oh, most assuredly!" Menge added quickly as his eyes were drawn again to the leather coverlet. "I couldn't agree more. Ah hahaha. Ah ha." His laughter, somehow, didn't sound quite natural. And when he looked into her eyes again, there was a new quality to his gaze, a certain pitifulness, like a naughty boy pleading with his mother for a favor. Mother Antoinette found she liked that quality a great deal.

"Antoinette," he said, quickly and urgently, "I need to talk to you. We must make our plans for conquest. With the chaos of the Change around us, the time is ripe for our success—and, once we defeat Dread, the Cineverse will be ours!''

Mother Antoinette smiled at that. It was rather charming when her Mengy tried to be forceful. ''I have my own plans for conquest,'' she replied, her eyes traveling up and down Menge's silver uniform. ''I can't think of a better place and time for us to have our little talk.'' She flicked her whip for emphasis. The point snicked out to caress Menge's shoulder.

CRACK

''No better place?'' Mengy looked down at the tear in his silver suit. ''Oh. Perhaps not.''

She stepped forward quickly, placing her hand over the rent in Menge's silver garb. The hard leather had cut cleanly through the fabric, but she had enough control of the whip by now not to break the skin. She rubbed her whip-calloused palm against the newly revealed smoothness of Menge's shoulder.

Mengy's pencil-thin mustache quivered uncontrollably. When he spoke, his voice was a husky croak.

''Antoinette!''

She pulled him to her.

There was a knock on the door.

Mengy blinked and pulled himself away. The spell was broken.

''Who could that be?'' he asked, his voice squeaking with dismay. ''Our plans must be secret! The future of the Cineverse depends upon it.'' His head whipped back and forth to take in the entire room. ''I have to hide!''

Hide? Oh, very well. The spell might be broken at the moment, but she could certainly save him for later. She looked about the room for a hiding place. Menge's tummy, unfortunately, made him a bit too large to fit under the bed. However, one of the closets would do nicely.

She pointed to the left-hand closet—the one with the tapestry of the landlord forcing the debtor family out into the snow.

''In there!'' she commanded. ''Quickly!''

Menge hurried to obey. Mother Antoinette crossed the room quickly, her heels clacking as sharply as gunfire.

"Who disturbs me?" she demanded of the solid and still closed door.

"This is not one of your wimpy males," a gruff female voice answered. "This is Big Bertha, seeking an audience that might be to our mutual advantage!"

Bertha? This could prove interesting. Besides, now that Antoinette had made her intentions clear, it might do Mengy good to spend some time in that closet. Anticipation, especially frustrated anticipation, could make things so much more intense.

She opened the door. Bertha stepped quickly into the room, her black vinyl jumpsuit doing little to hide the muscles bulging underneath. Still, Antoinette did not know if she approved of both of them wearing black. It was only a small step from vinyl to leather, after all, and that would never do. Antoinette hoped, at least for now, she could spare Bertha a lesson from the whip.

"I'm glad you're alone," Bertha remarked after a cursory glance around the room. She shut the door herself. "The Change is upon us, and, this time, it's going to change to our advantage!"

Mother Antoinette was curious despite herself. "What do you mean?"

"Dread and his ilk have no vision," Bertha replied. "He pursues the Change for his own limited ends. And, if he wins, what of it? One *man* will replace another as ruler of the Cineverse. And we women will be left behind." Her huge hands balled into fists, twin jackhammers ready to destroy—until the frown of distaste on her countenance was abruptly replaced by the slightest of smiles. "But not anymore. The first time I saw you, I knew you were different. I knew you were the first woman worthy to conquer at Bertha's side." She allowed herself a short, harsh laugh. "Together, we can prove that women can be as cruel, heartless, and despicable as men. And, once we have won, we will be able, at our leisure, to bend males to our will." Her hands opened to grasp at the riches that would someday be theirs.

Mother Antoinette took a deep breath. What Big Bertha said made a great deal of sense. Perhaps it was the fact that Bertha was so forcefully direct, with none of the pregnant pauses her male counterparts so favored; perhaps it was Antoinette's new surroundings, or the reassuring feel of the whip in her hand—but, whatever had changed, it meant that, more than ever before, something inside Antoinette felt like this was her turn for conquest. At last, her time had come.

But then, why was there something else inside her that fought against this?

It had something to do with Roger, didn't it? her undutiful son. She looked again at Bertha's grasping hands and hungry eyes. Bertha had more than a need to control; she had a need to devour. Antoinette knew, from earlier, unpleasant discussions, how Bertha felt about her son, and she had no doubt, should she help Bertha gain control of the Cineverse, one of the first to be devoured would be Roger.

But why should that bother her? Her son never called, never wrote, never introduced her to any of his women friends unless he was about to get married to one of them. He had always been terrible about cleaning up his room, his clothes never made it into the hamper, she could forget about him even touching a dirty dish, and he hadn't even said thank you when she had given away all those old things of his that had needlessly been cluttering up her house for years. Why shouldn't she be eager to see someone as inconsiderate as that be devoured?

But there was another voice, very small, very deep inside her, that whispered oh-so-faintly: "No, not Roger!" So small, but so insistent.

As unpleasant as this was, she had to face it. Mother Antoinette was still a mother.

"Well?" Bertha demanded. "What do you say?"

Antoinette frowned. She did not approve of anyone else—even someone as large and politically persuasive as Bertha—making demands. Before her recent transformation, Antoinette had spent her entire life acceding to others' wishes. Now, she had a few wishes of her own.

"I must consider—" she began.

She was interrupted by a knock on the door.

"Who could that be?" Bertha demanded with an edge of panic. "We must not be discovered together before we can adequately plan!" She looked around for some means of escape. "I will have to hide!"

She glanced underneath the bed, but dismissed the space as much too narrow for her bulk. She started instead toward the landlord tapestry, but Antoinette gently redirected her toward the opposite closet, and the wall-hanging of Lucretia Borgia.

"It's so much more appropriate," Antoinette murmured softly but urgently.

Bertha replied with a businesslike nod, and marched to the other corner of the room.

The knocker knocked again, more insistently this time. Mother Antoinette realized she had to deal with this directly. She spun and headed quickly for the door again, her heels pounding as hard as a carpenter driving nails into a coffin.

When she spoke, her words were clipped as sharp as daggers. "Who dares to bother me?"

"It is I!" an imperious voice blustered on the other side of the door. "Your leader! Doctor Dread! Let me in"—he paused portentously— "please?"

Now it was this Dread person? She supposed she should open the door, if only in appreciation of the suite that he had arranged for her. But what if he desired more than a friendly chat? Her fingers tightened around the reassuring handle of her whip. If he had any other ideas, she would quickly change his mind.

She pulled the door open with a jerk.

"Mrs. Gor—" Dread hesitated in surprise. "I mean, Mother Antoinette. How nice of you to"—paused a bit more calmly as he stepped inside—"invite me in."

She regarded him coolly. "Yes, Doctor. What might I do for you?"

Dread avoided her eyes. "This is a very—delicate matter." He looked at their surroundings as if the walls might have ears.

"I don't know if you are"—he hesitated tellingly—"aware of the situation."

"If you say so," she replied noncomittally. She didn't want to show too much emotion until she could determine exactly what it was Dread was hesitating about.

The slightest of smiles fluttered about the Doctor's lips. It reminded Mother Antoinette of nothing so much as a ghostly pale moth somehow drawn to a flame and simultaneously frightened to show itself.

"The Change is"—he paused knowingly—"all around us."

"Yes?" Mother Antoinette prompted.

"The Change has"—Dread hesitated teasingly—"happened before. I know the signs."

"Do tell," Antoinette replied. She wished that she could somehow get Dread to hesitate a little less.

"I am"—Dread paused as the smile flickered across his lips again—"experienced in this sort of thing. I am"—his gaze caught Antoinette's for an instant before he nervously looked way—"experienced in so many things."

"So you say," Mother Antoinette managed. She tried to smile, but her teeth clamped together in a rictus grin. Perhaps, she thought, Doctor Dread had hesitated once too often.

"Yes"—Dread stopped to take a deep breath—"I do. But the Change has given me"—the words caught in his throat yet again—"beneficial experience," Dread managed before his next pause—"experience which would be to our mutual—"

This had gone too far. There was only so much Mother Antoinette could abide. It was time for the whip.

"—benefit," Dread managed as the whip leapt in Antoinette's hand.

CRACK

Dread's mouth fell open in an even more profound hesitation.

CRACK *CRACK* *CRACK*

The whip wrapped itself around Doctor Dread's snakeskin-clad shoulders. Mother Antoinette jerked him forward.

Dread's incredibly thin lips quivered, reminding Antoinette of nothing so much as a fish mouth longing for a worm. "Exactly—what I was—trying to say." Dread gasped with every pause. "With you—the Change—would be something special."

Something special? Mother Antoinette felt as if somebody had kicked in the ribs of her leather bustier. For once, she didn't know what to say.

She heard some sort of growl from the closets behind her. Could it be Menge, vocalizing some jealous rage, or Bertha, forced to comment on Doctor Dread's blatantly male tactics?

Dread had heard it, too.

"What was that?" he demanded, for once not hesitating at all.

Mother Antoinette realized that to master this situation she needed whiplike speed in her mind as well. What kind of explanation would a man with Dread's background accept? Perhaps something from a soap opera would be melodramatic enough, or the sort of thing she found in those fiction supplements at the back of women's magazines.

"Only the sound of my startled heart," she replied, as she did her best to stare demurely at the floor. Still, she wasn't sure words like that quite fit, here in the Citadel of Dread. Besides which, it wasn't all that easy to look demure when you were holding a whip.

"Really?" Dread answered uncertainly, as if—as she feared—he was not quite ready to accept the explanation. "But—"

How dare he object so blatantly? Mother Antoinette found herself suddenly angry that this snakeskin-covered toad would question her *heart*!

"And who are you," she retorted quickly, "to question *anything* that happens in my chamber?"

Doctor Dread took a wary step away, but, beyond clearing his throat, he offered no further opposition. He seemed much happier to accept her second, more violent response.

But what, she wondered, should she do for an encore?

She was saved by the explosion.

"Blue smoke?" Doctor Dread declared. "Who could it be? We can't be seen together like this. Not until you have made your"—this time, his hesitation sounded panic-stricken—"intentions clear!"

Mother Antoinette quietly suggested that Doctor Dread hide under the bed. She was glad she finally had someone svelte enough to fit down there. She hated to waste a good hiding place.

In the meantime, the blue smoke had started to clear.

"What's going on here?" a new voice shouted abruptly. "What has happened to my small yet economical headquarters?"

Mother Antoinette flicked her wrist.

CRACK went the whip. *CRACK* *CRACK* *CRACK*

"I was only asking!" the newcomer wailed. He was a compact fellow wearing army fatigues, but he also sported that pencil-thin mustache so favored by all the local men. Unlike Menge's stately rotundness, however, this fellow didn't seem to have an ounce of fat on his body, probably because—with the way he twitched and jerked about—he was never still enough for any fat to settle down. Mother Antoinette wondered idly how quick this one might be to dance to the song of her whip. She began to see a certain wisdom to Betha's thoughts on men.

The jerky newcomer stared intently at her. "You still haven't answered my question."

She certainly hadn't. She had learned her lesson with her recent experience with Doctor Dread. Now that she was Mother Antoinette, she had no need to make any explanations. Instead, she made a simple statement.

"Your headquarters are *my* headquarters now."

"Oh," was the newcomer's quiet reply. "It's all I could expect, the way things have been going. I don't suppose you know where I'm supposed to be?"

Mother Antoinette's only answer was a playful flick of her wrist. The whip danced mere inches from the newcomer's nose. But this new fellow was too preoccupied with his own thoughts to do more than flinch.

"I should have known it wasn't my day," the newcomer moaned. "First it was Mort the Killer Robot and Diablo, the Gorilla with the Mind of a Man! Then it was my deadly tank, with its uncounted tons of screaming metal destruction! And now my—room is gone?" He put his fist to his forehead as he choked back a sob. "How much turmoil can one villain abide?"

He certainly appeared to be a high-strung sort. And yet, in his groveling way, he seemed very sincere. Mother Antoinette had to admit it—you certainly met a lot of interesting men in the Cineverse. If only her bridge club could see her now! But she had left the bridge club far behind, along with the garden club, the civic association, and any other organization she couldn't control with the whip!

"But I am forgetting my villainous manners," the newcomer continued, trying to gain control over his emotions. "You may call me Peril. Professor Peril, specializing in badness on a budget."

She pointed at herself with the handle of her whip. "Mother Antoinette. Any questions?"

"Well—uh—yes," Peril managed. "What am I to do without my room?"

She continued to stare at him silently.

"Not that I suppose you would be interested in something as insignificant as that, Mother Antoinette," he added hastily. She continued to regard him without emotion.

"Not that I should presume to know what you might be interested in!" Peril added with a weak excuse for a smile.

Almost despite herself, her eyes fell on the leather-covered bed. "I have my priorities!"

"Your—" Peril's gaze followed her own. "The bed? The bed is very nice."

Mother Antoinette could hear muffled words coming from one of the closets and under the bed.

"What was that?" Peril shrieked. My, he was certainly a jumpy fellow.

"Drafts," was Mother Antoinette's unconcerned reply.

"Yes," Peril remarked absently. "I have noticed them myself. This citadel may be imposing, but it is anything but energy efficient." His eyes wandered back to the black leather spread. "That is a much nicer bed than I used to have."

This time, groans of protest came from all three hiding places.

"Are you sure there's no one else here?" Peril asked uncertainly.

Mother Antoinette shrugged her leather-clad shoulders. "Mice, perhaps."

"Mice?" Peril replied. "Oh, dear, no. Most definitely rats. Norwegian rats. Doctor Dread had them imported, you know, to give the citadel a touch of—"

Mother Antoinette had had enough of talk. It was time for action. As usual, her whip spoke for her.

CRACK

Peril stared at the leather thong newly hugging his trim midsection. When he spoke again, there was wonder in his voice:

"Mother Antoinette. You make me feel like a giddy schoolboy. Something has gone out of my life since that ape and robot vanished. With you, though, it could happen all over again. I could have a sense of style!"

The exclamations were getting louder from the hiding places:

"What?" "How dare—" "Who does he—"

"Is it something about the acoustics in here?" Peril asked with a frown.

But Mother Antoinette was unhappy as well. She had not asked to be disturbed by any of these intruders, and she had

had enough of skulking in closets. When she wanted something, she wanted it now.

Again the whip moved, almost of its own volition.

CRACK *CRACK* *CRACK*

Both tapestries were flung aside as the whip shot to either side of the bed.

"Oh, my," Menge muttered distractedly. "I must have made a wrong turn. How could I possibly—"

"Oh, there you are, Antoinette dearest," Bertha said quickly. "I do think it's time we had a—"

But the whip was not finished with its mischief.

CRACK *CRACK* *CRACK*

Antoinette jerked the handle, and the whip-wrapped Doctor Dread came rolling out from underneath the bed.

But their leader showed none of the apology or surprise of his fellows. Instead, he appeared livid, his crimson face badly clashing with his green snakeskin cowl.

"How dare you disturb me in the middle of an—er—inspection!" he demanded. "I have heard you have—rats here. That's it!" He sat up and looked at the rest of the assemblage. "Rats!" He grabbed the whip in both of his hands and pulled. Under her startled gaze, the handle flew from Mother Antoinette's grip.

"Believe me, underlings!" Dread ranted. "There will be—changes made. There will be—dues to pay."

Mother Antoinette looked from face to face. None of them appeared happy, and her three fellow underlings even looked somewhat afraid.

"Guards!" Doctor Dread screamed.

Menge, Peril, and Bertha took a collective step backwards. Oh, dear, Antoinette thought. Without the whip in her hand and all—she hadn't felt this uncertain since her days on Earth.

Had she finally gone too far?

12

Roger coughed. Roger hacked. Roger couldn't get any oxygen. The combination of the smoke bomb and Professor Peril's blue-smoke disappearance seemed to have used up all the breathable air.

That's when the thunderous roar of industrial motors cut in, sounding like nothing so much as the propellers on a World War II fighter plane.

All the smoke disappeared as if by magic. Roger gulped a draft of clean air.

The Plotmaster still stood in the same, backlit spot, as if all the business with Professor Peril really hadn't affected him in the least. He chuckled.

PRETTY GOOD, HUH?
LUCKY FOR US I'VE GOT THOSE PROPELLERS FROM THOSE WORLD WAR II FIGHTER PLANES.

He paused to take a long, satisfied drag on his blue-smoke cigar.

IT'S ONE OF THE PERKS OF BEING THE PLOT-MASTER.
YOU GET TO KEEP SOME OF THE PROPS!

Roger shook his head. He felt like all this smoke had fogged his brain as well as clogged his lungs.

Dwight was barking his brains out, as if recent events were too much for even a Wonder Dog. Roger had to agree. The more time he spent with the Plotmaster, the less he seemed to understand.

"But, aren't you upset?" he asked. "The Professor just made good his escape!"

ROGER, BOOBALA!
THIS IS THE CINEVERSE—
MY CINEVERSE!
NOBODY ESCAPES UNLESS I WANT THEM TO!

"But I thought—" Roger began, not sure now what he had thought. The Plotmaster filled in for him:

THAT THINGS WERE OUT OF CONTROL?

The Plotmaster paused an instant to puff thoughtfully on his cigar.

WELL, MAYBE THEY ARE, SORT OF—
THE CINEVERSE IS A BIG PLACE.
TOO BIG, PERHAPS, EVEN FOR THE PLOTMASTER!

The backlit guy in blue was interrupted by a blast from the heavenly choir. The Plotmaster glared overhead.

I DIDN'T ASK FOR ANY COMMENTS FROM YOU!
YOUR JOB'S ON THE LINE HERE!

The angelic choir was instantly silent. He turned back to Roger, his voice again cheerful and in control.

THAT BIT WITH—WHAT WAS HIS NAME?
OH, YEAH—PROFESSOR PERIL.
SOMETIMES, THESE VILLAINS . . .

He chuckled, leaving the rest of his thought unsaid.
"But the bomb!" Roger objected. "And Peril's escape!"
The Plotmaster chuckled again.

OH YEAH, THAT STUFF WITH THE SMOKE BOMB!
I WAS PRETTY GOOD, WASN'T I?
AND NEVER A DAY OF DRAMATIC TRAINING!

He waved the sheaf of papers in his hand for emphasis.

I TELL YOU, THE PLOTMASTER
IS ALWAYS READY FOR CHANGES IN THE SCRIPT!

"Changes?" Roger asked hopelessly, "—in the script?"
The Plotmaster shook his head sympathetically.

YOU THOUGHT THE SCRIPT ALWAYS STAYED THE SAME?
WELL, MAYBE IT DID ONCE—
BUT NOT SINCE THE CHANGE!

He waved the pages in his hands for emphasis.
Roger noticed the heavenly choir was back again, this time humming softly—yet inspirationally—in the background.

BUT THERE ARE STILL WAYS TO CONTROL THE SCRIPT.
WAYS FOR THE PLOTMASTER—
OR FOR CAPTAIN CRUSADER!

The Plotmaster coughed, and the heavenly music halted abruptly. He stared distractedly for a moment at his blue-smoke cigar.

BUT I'M GETTING AHEAD OF MYSELF HERE, AREN'T I?
YOU'LL HAVE TO FORGIVE AN OLD PLOTMASTER—
SO MANY PLOTS, SO LITTLE TIME!

He stuck the cigar back in his silhouetted mouth and began to page through the script.

YOU KNOW, OF COURSE, THAT I COULD HAVE CONTROLLED PROFESSOR PERIL.

The Plotmaster made this statement flatly, speaking around his cigar.

AND THE SMOKE BOMB?
TO ME IT WAS NOTHING MORE THAN
ANOTHER PLOT DEVICE.

The Plotmaster's head rose to regard Roger.

BUT GIVE PERIL HIS FREEDOM—
AND YOU'D BE SURPRISED WHAT HE'LL LEAD US TO!
EXCUSE ME FOR A SECOND.

He looked back down to the script.

WE JUST HAVE TO LOOK AHEAD HERE A COUPLE OF PAGES.

With a cry of triumph, he poked his forefinger at the top of the right-hand page.

HERE!
HE'S GONE TO THE CITADEL OF DREAD!
SEE HOW EASY THAT WAS?

"The Citadel of Dread?" Roger didn't particularly like the sound of that. Still, the Plotmaster seemed pretty pleased with himself.

YEAH,
I'M PRETTY IMPRESSED WITH IT MYSELF—
AND I PROBABLY INVENTED THE PLACE!

The blue embers glowed on the end of his cigar as the Plotmaster took a deep, satisfied breath.

THE CITADEL OF DREAD!
WHAT A PLACE TO HAVE THE CLIMAX,
HUH?

Roger felt a certain panic rising inside him. This was all going too fast for him. "Climax? Is it time for the climax?"

IS IT TIME?
OH, COME ON NOW, ROGER BABY,
DON'T YOU THINK THIS BUSINESS HAS GONE
FAR ENOUGH?

This business? Roger guessed the Plotmaster was talking about the Plotmaster and the Change. But there was a lot of other business that needed taking care of, too. What about Delores and the Slime Monster? What about his mother and the Zeta Ray? What about Big Louie and all the others stranded back on that Cop Movie world?

"Far enough?" Roger wondered aloud. "I guess so, except—"

The Plotmaster nodded knowingly.

YOU'RE WORRIED ABOUT THOSE
ERRANT PLOT THREADS, AREN'T YOU?
ROGER, BABE, TAKE IT FROM THE PLOTMASTER!
ONCE YOU GET TO THE CLIMAX,
THOSE PLOT THREADS HAVE A WAY OF SHOWING
UP!

Roger guessed he had to take the Plotmaster's word for it. Actually, so far, he had had to take the Plotmaster's word for everything.

The backlit man in blue leaned forward, his voice low, almost conspiratorial.

BESIDES, IT'S TIME FOR THE CHANGE,
AND THIS TIME, IT'S GONNA BE BIG!
WORLDS COLLIDE! CULTURES CLASH!

ACTION! ADVENTURE! COMEDY! ROMANCE!
I TELL YOU, ROGER BABY,
WHEN DOCTOR DREAD STARTED ALL THIS,
HE DIDN'T KNOW WHAT HE WAS GETTING INTO!
SOMETIMES, I WORRY ABOUT THE CHANGE.
BUT, THIS ONE?
WHAT A SPECTACLE IT'S GOING TO BE!

The Plotmaster leaned back and took a puff on his blue-smoke cigar.

AND, ROGER?
THIS IS FROM THE HEART,
I CERTAINLY HOPE YOU LIVE THROUGH IT!

Roger hoped so, too. He spoke with a certain resignation: "So I have to go to the Citadel of Dread?"

He sighed as he reached into his jacket pocket to pull out his cheap plastic means of transportation.

His pocket was empty.

"My ring!" he shouted. "What happened to my ring?"

The Plotmaster only laughed.

A RING?
WHO NEEDS A RING
WHEN YOU'RE CAPTAIN CRUSADER!

This was going beyond confusion. Angelic choir, blue smoke, and mysterious backlighting be damned—Roger was starting to get annoyed.

"But how do I get from world to world?" Roger demanded. "Do I still say 'See you in the funny papers'?"

THOSE ARE SIMPLY WORDS—
A MOVIE MANTRA FOR THOSE
NOT AS FOCUSED AS CAPTAIN CRUSADER.

"So you *don't* have to say 'See you in the funny papers'?" Roger insisted. He still wasn't getting any straight answers here. Come to think of it, in his last couple of trips through the Cineverse—to the Cop Movie world and then here, wherever it was that the Plotmaster called home—he hadn't said "See you in the funny papers!" once.

The Plotmaster made a noise deep in his throat.

THERE ARE AS MANY WORDS OF POWER IN THE CINEVERSE
AS THERE ARE MOVIE WORLDS.

He puffed on his blue-smoke cigar and tilted his head up in the general direction of his angelic choir, which had started in again.

"THERE'S NO PLACE LIKE HOME"
WAS ALWAYS A GOOD ONE
OR
"LET'S WIN ONE FOR THE GIPPER!"
BUT ALL THIS IS BESIDES THE POINT.
WE'VE HAD ENOUGH PLOT HERE FOR EVEN THE PLOTMASTER.
IT'S TIME FOR ACTION!

The Plotmaster pulled the blue-smoke cigar from his mouth and waved it as he spoke.

DON'T WORRY ABOUT THE MECHANICS!
ROGER. SWEETIE-BABY!
YOU SHOULD KNOW BY NOW
ABOUT MOVIE MAGIC!

"Oh, yeah," Roger replied, half to himself. Movie magic—like when he was on that Beach Party world, and had sung that surfing song to master that wave among waves, the Cowabungamunga.

"Movie magic." He whispered the words, as if speaking them aloud might give them too much power.

But, speaking of power, there seemed to be an awful lot

of blue smoke in the air, and all of it was coming from the Plotmaster's waving cigar.

I CERTAINLY HAVE ENJOYED OUR LITTLE CHAT,
ROGER BABY!
KNOCK 'EM DEAD
AT THE CITADEL OF DREAD!

So he was on his way, just like that? Roger wished he had the Plotmaster's confidence. Not only that, Roger wished he knew exactly what the Plotmaster expected him to do.

But it was too late for wishes. Roger was surrounded by blue smoke, and the fading words of the Plotmaster:

SEE YOU IN THE FUNNY PAPERS!

13

There was only the void, and the sound of a very angry chicken.

Delores had no idea where she was. One moment, she had been surrounded by the insane hum of the transmogrifier—the next, all was darkness.

"Brawwk!" the chicken screamed.

Maybe the bird's voice was a clue. Delores thought back to that awful, frightening moment, strapped into the machine, when she was bathed by blinding light. She had thought, then, that this might be—the end.

Perhaps she was right. Perhaps it was.

There had been so many different animals there at that last moment, a veritable Noah's Ark-worth of species crowded into that tiny transmogrification room. There had been bunnies and sheep, dogs, and cats, insects and—chickens. Maybe they had all perished in that instant, the sheer bulk of life in that room proving too great a burden for even a machine as frightening as the transmogrifier. Perhaps her soul had followed the animals into the afterlife. Perhaps she had gone to chicken heaven, and this darkness was nothing but an endless mound of seedcorn, blocking out the celestial sun.

"Brawwwwwk!" the chicken declared even more vehemently.

Delores realized that there was a problem with her theory. Why was this chicken angry if it was in heaven? She had an awful moment of realization. If chickens could go to heaven, what would prevent the fowl from going—elsewhere in the afterlife?

"Brawwk!" the chicken reasserted. "Braw—Braw—"

The enraged clucks turned to coughs. "Braw—Oh, dear. You'll have to excuse me. Something is not quite right."

Delores breathed in sharply. The chicken was speaking with the voice of Edward the Slime Monster. Well, whatever had happened to Edward, he'd better be able to answer some questions!

"Baahhh!" she began. Where had that come from? She had meant to ask "Where are we?" or some such.

Instead, she had bleated.

"Baahhh?" she repeated. At least this time, it sounded more like a question.

"I may have made a slight miscalculation," Edward admitted. "Bawwk," he added.

Delores felt suddenly cold. She hugged her arms close to her body, her hands digging deep into her luxurious thick wool coat.

There was something else wrong here. Why should she be cold if she was wearing a heavy wool coat? But, now that she thought of it, she hadn't been wearing any coat at all—before the transmogrification.

What had the Slime Monster done to her?

"Baaahhhhhh!" she bleated in terror.

"Then again," Edward admitted, "I may have made a major miscalculation."

Delores couldn't stand this. If Edward was talking, why couldn't she? She would simply have to try harder.

"Bah—" she began, using all her concentration to get her lips, or whatever was now where her lips used to be, to form words and sentences. "B-b-but—" she managed at last, "wa-wa-where ar-r-re we?"

"Bawwwwk?" Edward replied in surprise. "Oh. I think we are somewhere in that lightless and formless void that exists beyond and between the worlds of the Cineverse, a place of total silence and darkness."

This was the sort of thing Delores was afraid of. "T-total darkness?" she repeated, mostly to make sure her newly recovered voice was still working.

"Yes," Edward answered, "so it is said, except for ancient legends that declare, should you travel far enough within the void, you might find a small, bright red sign with but a single word: EXIT."

"Exit?" Delores asked, feeling that she was finally gaining some control over her voice. Still, there was something about that single word that she found every bit as disquieting as everything else around here. Somehow, "Exit" sounded an awful lot like "The End."

Now that she had her voice, though, maybe she could finally ask some of those questions bursting inside her, like, first and foremost:

"Edward, how do you know abahhh—er—about all this sort of thing?"

"Voluminous research. When you're a slime monster, you have a very limited social life. This leaves you with a lot of free time."

This, at least, made sense. Delores fully agreed that the Slime Monster could use some help with his social skills. But somehow she felt that etiquette lessons would not help them out of their present situation. She asked her second question:

"Edward, why did we end up here?"

The Slime Monster paused a moment before answering this time.

"It had something to do with the transmogrifier—I think. That, and all the various species that crowded into the room as the transmogrification began. I'm afraid—bawwwk—that we've brought a few of the animals along with us, in a way—bawwwk—that I hadn't planned. It could be that the load of animals was too much for the transmogrifier to take, that the very experiment was too much for even the world of the Institute of Very Advanced Science to accept. After transmogrification, we could now be so different that there might not be a single world in the Cineverse that could accept us."

So different? Delores thought about her new, and very attached, wool coat. Now that she considered it, maybe this lightless (and even more importantly, mirrorless) void was a blessing in disguise.

"Then again," Edward further mused, "perhaps this is not some strange quirk of fate. Perhaps this is meant to be, and our present state is but another stage of the transmogrification."

"You mean the process—might not be finished yet?" Delores found she was even more frightened than she had been before.

"Bawwwwwk!" Edward replied. "All I can say is what I said to you before has come true—we are now united in a way that few people—or slime monsters, for that matter—will ever know." He made a noise deep in his throat, half sigh, half cluck. "I will admit, though, that it isn't quite what I expected."

"Bahhhhh!" Delores agreed.

"And I thought this would be the perfect world!" Edward lamented. "I'm so annoyed I could just peck!"

Delores guessed she could relate to that. She knew she would feel much better if she just had a little grass to chew on.

They both stood for a moment in truly total silence.

"If this is a new stage of the transmogrification," Edward ventured at last, "it's as boring as the last phase was overwhelming. We must, somehow, find our way back into the Cineverse."

Delores felt something brush against her arm, and then a hand closed around her own—a hand seemingly covered with very damp feathers.

"Come, Delores," the Slime Monster intoned. "I think it's time we looked for that exit."

14

"Zabana see light!"

Louie squinted. Yes, there was a point of light in the distance, like the end to a long tunnel. Perhaps, he thought, they hadn't traveled all the way to the true Pit of Absurdity. But what could be more absurd than their present situation?

After being unceremoniously dumped down here by the various relatives of ancient gods and heroes, Louie had landed softly and unscathed on something that felt like a thick bed of moss. He had quickly checked that all his fellows were similarly unhurt, and suggested they find a way out of this dramatically dark place. It seemed to Louie that there had been an awful lot of dramatically dark places in their recent travels. Undoubtedly it had something to do with the Change.

It was then that Zabana had seen the light. The best thing to do, Louie decided, was to approach the illumination. If nothing else, they would be able to see.

Doc, Officer O'Clanrahan, Zabana, and Louie all moved cautiously through the gloom. Well, Louie guessed he was doing his sidekick job; the plot was certainly moving right along. With the Change in full swing, though, it was impossible to guess where the plot might be going.

They had wanted to end up on one world, after all, and had found themselves somewhere completely different, and, instead of cute bunnies, they had been confronted by massive musclemen. Louie doubted he'd made a mistake with the ring. He was too practiced a sidekick for that sort of error. Instead, he considered it far more likely that the Change had altered the very fabric of the Cineverse!

"What that?" Zabana demanded.

"What's what?" Louie asked, increasingly perplexed with the direction all this was taking.

"Strange noise," Zabana insisted. "Something down here with us."

Louie didn't hear anything, but he had no reason to doubt Zabana's jungle-trained senses.

"Tarnation!" Doc exclaimed. "Do you think my six-shooters would work down here?"

"Why don't we take that ring of yours and go someplace a little more friendly?" Officer O'Clanrahan suggested a little shakily. Louie didn't think he'd ever seen such a change in a man—the policeman had lost all his confidence. Without Dwight the Wonder Dog, O'Clanrahan didn't seem to be the same police officer.

Zabana's voice cut through the gloom:

"It closer now."

But what had Zabana's jungle-trained senses detected? They had already faced a slime monster in similar circumstances. This certainly couldn't be any worse—could it?

Then Louie heard it, too.

Thump.

The sound was soft, but close. Louie wondered if something was following them.

O'Clanrahan muttered from where he walked behind the others.

Thump thump.

It was louder this time, and somehow percussive. Louie wondered if it might be the distant pounding of some jungle drum, carried to them by the strange acoustics of the chamber around them.

O'Clanrahan said something else just below the level of Louie's hearing.

Thump thump thump.

It sounded like it was all around them now. Louie realized he'd been acting too much like a sidekick again—or, more precisely, he had been *reacting*, which, after all, was a sidekick's basic job. But, if they were going to succeed in their battle against Doctor Dread, one of them would have to lead, and somehow, Louie felt he was the best one here for the job. He supposed that stranger things had happened with the Change.

But where would he lead them? Exactly where were they, and where should they go? Louie had to think. There might be a clue in the name—the Pit of Absurdity.

Thump, went something much too close. Thump, thump, thump.

The noise had become quite regular now. Thump, thump, thump, thump. Perhaps, Louie thought, they were not in some sort of cave or tunnel, but inside a living organism. Could that thumping be the beating of a giant heart? That would certainly be properly absurd.

But if Louie's latest thought was true, the heart was speeding up.

Thumpthumpthump thump, came the ever-increasing beat. Thumpthumpthumpthumpthumpthump thumpthump-thump. The echoes in this place made it sound like the noises were coming from everywhere. Unless, of course, the noises *were* coming from everywhere.

Whether he was going to be a sidekick or a leader, Louie knew there was only one thing to do.

"Run!" he yelled to the others. "Let's get out into the light!"

They ran, their pounding feet surrounded and lost within the noise of a hundred thumps. But they had almost reached the light. Louie could see his fellows running beside him as the illumination filtered into the tunnel. And he saw something else as well. They were not alone.

They were surrounded by bunnies.

"Whoo-eee!" Doc yelped. "Everybody's animated!"

Louie realized that they had reached their destination after all. He grinned at Zabana and Doc. For some reason, O'Clanrahan looked even more upset than he had before. Was the Change getting to be too much for the elderly police officer? At the rate things were moving now, Louie guessed he could really empathize with the cop's confusion. But, as far as he was concerned, that confusion ended here.

"Okay, guys!" he yelled to the non-bunnies as they all ran out under the cartoon sun. "Enough's enough! Let's stop running already!"

"But we like to run!" cheered a gray and white bunny that Louie recognized—was his name Fluffytail? "And hop and jump and skip and romp and cavort—"

"Running can be nice," Louie interrupted after he had taken a second to catch his breath. "But we have a job to do!"

"Job?" a much deeper voice asked as a much larger (approximately six-foot-high) rabbit bounded forward. Louie remembered this one, too.

"Bouncer!" the very large rabbit introduced himself anyway. "Bouncer likes jobs. Bouncer can harvest carrots. Bouncer can gather lettuce."

"Well," Louie replied, "this is a rather special job."

"Bouncer can pick broccoli!" the large rabbit insisted.

"Broccoli?" the Prince of the Jungle perked up. "Zabana like broccoli!"

"Bunnies like all sorts of vegetables!" Fluffytail explained. "Carrots and lettuce and broccoli and cauliflower and brussel sprouts and Hubbard squash and water chestnuts—"

Big Louie couldn't allow himself to be distracted.

"This has nothing to do with vegetables," he interrupted again, trying to keep the exasperation out of his voice. "But it really is a job that only bunnies can do."

"Bunnies are Zabana's friends!" the jungle prince added helpfully.

"It is only with your help," Louie continued, "that we can hope to defeat"—he paused appropriately— "Doctor Dread."

"Doctor Dread?" asked another one of the bunnies, whose name might have been Spottynose or Bentear or something like that. "Who's Doctor Dread?"

"Bouncer likes Zabana, too!" The very large rabbit extended a welcoming paw, which the jungle prince regarded with great interest.

Who's Doctor Dread? Now Louie was confused. The last time they had been in these parts, the bunnies had spent all their time tormenting the snakeskin-suited villain with cream pies and exploding carrots. How could the bunnies not know Doctor Dread when they had spent so long fighting him?

But Fluffytail thumped his right rear paw in comprehension. "You mean Malevelo!"

Of course! How could Louie have forgotten? When Doctor Dread was on the Bunnyland world, he didn't wear snakeskin, he wore wizard's robes! This animated world was, after all, the place where Doctor Dread fit in all too well, and, instead of controlling the forces in the Cineverse, he found himself being controlled. Just as Captain Crusader had been transformed into the beach bunny Dee Dee Davenport on the surfing world, so was Doctor Dread totally changed on this bunny planet, becoming the easily angered but thoroughly ineffectual wizard Malevelo!

"Yes," Big Louie agreed. "Malevelo."

All the bunnies booed and hissed.

The jungle prince broke his pensive silence. "Broccoli is Zabana's friend, too."

"Broccoli is nice and green," Bouncer agreed with an eager nod.

"Also good source of calcium," Zabana added. He shook the bunny's paw at last.

Louie was impressed. The jungle prince and the very large rabbit seemed to have found a strange, intellectual rapport. Well—now that he looked at the two of them again—maybe not intellectual.

"Faith and begorrah!" Officer O'Clanrahan interjected in a brittle voice. "Shouldn't we be gettin' a move on?"

Even in a world as animated as this, Big Louie could still sense the officer's discomfort. Perhaps, if Louie could take a little time away from his leadership role to pursue more of his natural sidekick duties, he might be able to determine what was bothering the policeman. But sidekicking, and Officer O'Clanrahan's discomfort, would have to wait until they had defeated Doctor Dread. Besides which, Louie had to admit, O'Clanrahan was right. Now that they'd met the bunnies, there was no time for delay.

"Well, what do you say, bunnies?" he called to the assembled rabbithood. "We need you to come with us, so that we can defeat Doctor Dread, stop the Change, and save the Cineverse!"

"Tarnation!" Doc exclaimed. "Now *that's* a summary!"

Louie allowed himself the slightest of smiles. At least he could still fit some of his sidekick talents in.

"With a summary like that," Fluffytail agreed, "how could any creatures as warm and cuddly and fluffy and cute and loyal and true as bunnies possibly say no?"

The other bunnies cheered.

"We'll all go!" Fluffytail announced, and his fellows cheered a second time.

Officer O'Clanrahan leaned close to Louie's ear. "Saints alive! We can't take all of them! And do we dare to take them from here?"

Louie nodded. Officer O'Clanrahan may have been a worrier, but both his objections were well taken. With the Change happening all around them, it was wise to expose themselves to as few risks as possible. As light as the bunnies were, they certainly couldn't take all of them. In fact, Louie guessed, from what he knew about Cineverse ring theory and the current weight of his comrades, they couldn't accommodate more than a dozen of their fluffy friends—considerably less if Bouncer was one of the chosen bunnies.

It was O'Clanrahan's second point, though, that really caused Louie concern. A simple review of the facts showed that when they attempted to reach Bunnyland, they had shown up on a muscleman planet that had somehow gotten itself attached. Now, if they left directly from the bunny world, would the Change allow them to reach their next destination, or send them someplace else altogether? Perhaps it would be best if they returned to the point on the muscleman world where they had come in. Using the ring there seemed to minimize complications, didn't it?

This was all too complicated for a sidekick to handle!

Louie felt his brain overloading. He wanted to stop where he was, and not do a thing until the hero showed up.

But the hero was gone, and Louie had to take over. He had to force himself to move and make a decision.

If he didn't, both Doctor Dread and the Change would win.

15

Dread stared at his henchmen. Professor Peril, Menge the Merciless, and Big Bertha all stared at Mother Antoinette. Except, now that she had lost her whip, she didn't feel like much of a mother anymore. In fact, Antoinette hadn't experienced anywhere near this sort of tension since her dear husband had passed away.

In the silence, she could hear the heavy boots of Dread's guards stomping down the hallway toward them.

"Wait a second!" Professor Peril interrupted. "Can't you see what's happening?"

"Certainly I can see!" Dread retorted with a harsh laugh. "You are to be"—he hesitated meaningfully—"dealt with. You are to be"—he paused tellingly—"taken care of."

"But why?" Peril shot back. "Don't you see what has taken place here? I come back to the Citadel of Dread, the greatest repository of evil in all the known Cineverse, and what do I find? People hiding in closets and under the bed! This does not sound like what should happen on a world famed for suspense and treachery! No, it sounds to me far more like"—it was his turn to pause, the mouth beneath his pencil-thin mustache twisting into a triumphant grin—"Screwball Comedy."

Doctor Dread's mouth fell open, his anger replaced by total shock. "Screwball—" he began.

It was then that the guards chose to break down the door, a half-dozen burly men in uniform, led by another whose suit was so festooned with medals and gold braid that he had to be their captain.

"Halt and surrender!" the Captain of the Guard called out. "In the name of Doctor Dread! There is no mercy in this citadel, and no hope for those who oppose it! Stand where you are, and face your obliteration like the scum—''

Doctor Dread cleared his throat. ''Captain? If I might interrupt?''

The Captain of the Guard snapped to attention. ''Yessir, Your Vileness!''

''Aren't you talking a bit much''—Dread hesitated as he stared at the knuckles of his snakeskin glove—''before you *deal* with the prisoners?''

''S-sorry, Your Corruptness,'' the Captain of the Guard stammered. ''It's just that, as a villain in good standing, I have to explain my actions at some length, especially before I obliterate someone—''

''It *is* a Law of the Cineverse,'' Professor Peril pointed out.

''And, well—'' The Captain of the Guard paused as he stared down at the newly polished marble floor. ''It's just that I get to say these dramatically charged things so seldom, what with the fearsome reputation this place has, and we guards have so few opportunities to strike terror into the hearts of interlopers, much less that all important opportunity to obliterate them—''

''Perhaps''—Doctor Dread interrupted and hesitated almost simultaneously—''we should wait a bit before we perform any—obliteration.'' He turned back to Professor Peril. ''Screwball—Comedy, did you say?''

Peril answered with a smug nod. ''People hiding in closets and under the bed? What else would you call it?''

''Like a''—Dread paused thoughtfully—''Screwball *Bedroom* Comedy?''

''Here? At the Citadel of Dread? The very heart of evil incarnate?'' Menge's eyes grew wide with terror. His voice quavered as he spoke: ''But that means—''

''The Change!'' Big Bertha finished for him.

''Yes, it is here, too.'' Doctor Dread nodded his snakeskin-cowled head solemnly. ''No place in the Cineverse—not even our beloved citadel—is—immune to the Change!''

Mother Antoinette looked from face to face. Everyone else seemed rather upset, didn't they? And all about some sort of change. She herself had been here such a short time, she wouldn't recognize any sort of change unless it came up and bit her. Which, she realized abruptly, could actually happen (the biting, that is) in a place like this.

In the midst of all this chaos, however, there was one thing she was certain of—that everything would be fine the moment she got her whip back.

"Which means"—Doctor Dread continued with the requisite hesitation—"that I must reconsider my actions."

"No obliteration, Your Surliness?" The Captain of the Guard could not keep the disappointment out of his voice.

Doctor Dread glanced at the others. "No—at least not at present."

Everyone sighed, the Captain and his guards from frustration, everyone else from relief.

"Have no fear!" their snakeskin-suited leader added quickly. "The way our plot is progressing, you will have no end of obliteration ahead of you."

The Captain of the Guard looked up at Doctor Dread, a glimmer of hope again in his gaze. "Do you really think so, Your Dreadfulness?"

"Oh, yes. And more than obliteration, too. There will be plenty of time for"—he paused to savor every word—"freelance pillaging, diabolical laughter, and general humiliation of the enemy!"

"Really?" The Captain of the Guard saluted sharply as he snapped to attention. "Oh, Your Hideousness! I knew I wouldn't be sorry when I signed up at the Citadel of Dread."

"No sir, Captain," Doctor Dread replied smoothly but slowly. "Now, if you and your guard—retire, I must—discuss my future plans with my—elite associates."

He turned back to the others in the room, a grin spread across his hawklike countenance. Apparently, Antoinette realized, they had all been forgiven.

Why didn't this turn of events make her feel more relieved? She was still so uncertain.

"Our time"—the bad doctor paused in a studied sort of way—"is limited. Those of you who were here the last time will remember the symptoms—movie worlds shifting and combining, all of the Cineverse thrown into chaos. Except this time—according to our plans, it will be much worse. As the Change progresses, it will be our task to make sure that certain worlds and individuals—namely us—remain triumphant. To that end, it is time to send—some of you—on a mission."

"Mission?" Professor Peril perked up. "That's what I like—action, and plenty of it!"

"Excellent," Doctor Dread purred. "Then you will not mind going to a certain place to remove certain pesky—" He paused again, although this time it seemed not so much for dramatic effect as for a genuine difficulty to speak the next two words that issued from his mouth.

"Fl-fluffy—" he managed at last, "b-bun-bun-bunnies!"

"Bunnies?" Antoinette asked doubtfully. "How do I kill bunnies?"

But Doctor Dread's oily smile was already back in place. "Alas, Mother Antoinette, I think we would be better served if you stayed"—he paused suggestively—"behind. There is much"—he stopped insinuatingly—"planning to be done." His hand snaked out to stroke her black leather glove. "Perhaps—we can discuss our—more personal future plans."

"What gives you—" Menge the Merciless began.

"Still throwing your weight—" Professor Peril muttered.

"Men!" Bertha somehow managed to spit out the word, even though it contained no *s* sounds.

All three paused abruptly after a glance at the still-present guards. Doctor Dread smiled and continued his attentions.

Antoinette stared down at the snakeskin-covered fingers playing about her wrist. What exactly was this man implying? She only knew one thing for certain—there was but a single way she could handle this.

She pulled her arm away.

"Only if you give me back my whip," was her reply.

Doctor Dread frowned for an instant, then shrugged. "If—you insist. Perhaps there is a place for—your whip in our—future as well."

Mother Antoinette's fingers closed around the reassuringly solid whip handle. She felt a certain peace and determination flood into her soul with that weight back in her hand, but more than that, too. She knew who she was now, and where she was going.

"I'll say there's a place for my whip!" she shouted with a laugh.

CRACK the whip danced. *CRACK* *CRACK*!

Doctor Dread leapt away as the Captain and all his guards hastily fled the room.

"Mother Antoinette!" their leader demanded. "What do you—intend to do?"

She paused to look at the man in snakeskin green. After his recent actions, did he deserve an answer? And what of the others? Did speedy Peril, strong Bertha, and even her beloved, cowering Mengy, deserve an explanation? Part of her wanted the others to know everything that was welling within her, but how could mere words do justice to what she was feeling?

She decided it was time to let her whip do her talking for her.

CRACK *CRACK* *CRACK*

The leather thong struck, first at the left, then the right side, of Dread's pencil-thin mustache, trimming away the errant hairs. The Doctor's mouth opened in amazement as Antoinette studied her handiwork. Her tonsorial efforts weren't quite as even as she might have liked, but she was getting better control with every passing moment. This whip was no longer a mere tool in her hand—it was an extension of her very being.

CRACK

Doctor Dread covered his upper lip and whimpered.

CRACK *CRACK*

Menge, Peril, and Bertha all covered various vulnerable parts of their anatomies.

CRACK *CRACK* *CRACK*

Mother Antoinette smiled. She had found her place in the Cineverse at last. And with her place, she had once again found her voice as well.

"So, Doctor Dread," she said slowly, each word weighted by her crimson lips, "you wished to have some—private words?"

"Oh, dear. Perhaps"—Doctor Dread flinched as he hesitated—"it would be a better idea for you to—go with the others."

"Never!" Peril blurted. "Don't change because—"

"Oh, no!" Menge interjected. "Your needs come—"

"We wouldn't think of depriving you—" Bertha added.

All three of them stopped as Antoinette smiled in their direction. The tail of the whip undulated in her hand like a living thing.

"Oh, Mother Antoinette," Peril began in an uncertain voice, "most certainly, if you'd like to come along—"

"So sorry," Menge quickly added. "We misunderstood—"

Bertha nodded eagerly. "We're ready to go any time *you're* ready!"

Doctor Dread cleared his throat, apparently trying to regain some of his villainous composure. "Very well. You know what to do. Take one of your rings and"—his voice died as he swallowed—"and—go."

He lifted a fist into the air, and forced himself to continue. "Deal with the b-bun—bun—" Doctor Dread took a deep breath. "Make sure—certain animals are taken care of, like b-bun—b-b-bun—" He shook his head to rid himself of the stutter. "There is no more time for hesitation when it comes to b-bu-bu—" He raised both fists in the air. "Obliterate them!"

Professor Peril took the lead. "Very well. Gather around—all of you." He waited until Menge, Bertha, and

Antoinette had grabbed onto his army fatigues. "See you in the funny papers!"

Mother Antoinette frowned. There was that blue smoke again. How could she control the Cineverse if she didn't know where the blue smoke came from?

But, even as her world was lost in roiling blue, she knew the answer was in her hand. The whip was an excellent tool to loosen tongues, and it would never leave her grip again! Woe be to the individual who tried—man or woman, from that master of evil, Doctor Dread, all the way down to her ineffectual son, Roger!

"Here come the bunnies!" Peril announced as the smoke started to clear.

"Kill them quickly," Bertha instructed. "And, whatever you do, don't look at their large, pink, incredibly trusting eyes."

"It's best you don't look too closely at their wonderfully soft fur, either," Menge added. He sounded much more like his old self, because, Mother Antoinette surmised, they were once again about to face action. Either that, or the blue smoke prevented him from staring at her whip.

"Yeah," Peril added grimly. "I'd also advise you to keep away from any study of their amazingly adorable pink paw-pads."

"Or their constantly moving and oh-so-cuddly noses," Menge continued painfully.

"And those fuzzy and fluffy pointy little ears," Bertha concluded between gritted teeth.

"It's tough being a villain," Peril summarized for all of them. "Stomping bunnies is the ultimate test."

Mother Antoinette curled the whip around both of her hands as the last of the smoke cleared. It was a test she would have to be ready for.

And then the smoke was gone. But there didn't seem to be any bunnies. Instead, there was a big rock, with three large, heavily muscled men—and you could see *all* their muscles with what little they were wearing—in front of it.

"Halt!" one of the magnificently muscled men called out

as he raised his sword. "In the name of Hippolita!"

Peril looked quickly at his fellows. "What do we do about this? This place looks prehistoric. Our weapons will never work here!"

Mother Antoinette stepped forward. "There's nothing wrong with my whip!"

"*Halt* we said," one of the musclemen repeated. "Or face the combined might of the son of Samson, the nephew of Hercules, and the second cousin of Goliath!"

Menge laid a hand on Antointte's leather-clad shoulder. "Can your whip handle all three of them?"

She glanced disdainfully at the hand on her shoulder. Menge quickly jerked his fingers back. She stepped forward, eager to see how far her whip could take her.

16

The noise alone was enough to freeze his bones.

Even though he was still surrounded by the Plotmaster's blue smoke, Roger could tell he had reached the new world from the sound of the wind. It howled about him, first soft and mournful, like a creature in pain, then loud and discordant, like a chorus of the doomed. It was the loneliest sound he had ever heard, and it reminded him that he had been sent to face Doctor Dread—alone.

He felt a great hopelessness weigh down his arms and legs, as if the wind were pressing him into the earth. What could he, Roger Gordon, public relations man from Earth, do against the ultimate master of evil?

But before he could have another depressing thought, the insistent wind blew the smoke away, and he saw he was on a gray, rocky plane, standing next to a dog.

"Bark! Yip! Bark!" The white German shepherd by his side wagged its tail enthusiastically.

Roger had almost forgotten—he wasn't alone. Dwight was here, too. The Plotmaster had rescued both of them, along with Professor Peril, from a watery grave, and it only made sense that the Plotmaster would send both of them here. And it wasn't simply Roger Gordon, or a simple canine, who now faced the forces of evil. It was the new Captain Crusader, with his trusty helper, Dwight the Wonder Dog.

"Think good thoughts," Roger mused aloud, "and good things happen." There. He felt better already—like somebody who could be Captain Crusader.

"Yip, arf arf!" Dwight agreed.

At least, agreement was what Roger thought Dwight was

trying to communicate. Now that he considered it, his relationship with this dog was a little frustrating. After all, both Louie and the Plotmaster seemed to be able to tell outright what Dwight was saying. Shouldn't Captain Crusader be able to do the same?

Well, maybe Roger shouldn't rush that sort of thing—he seemed to find new dimensions to his emerging hero status with every passing adventure. The ability to talk to animals could show up at any moment.

"Bark Bark yip!" Dwight interjected. Roger looked down to see that the dog was pointing like a hunting hound, his nose showing Roger the way to—what? Roger turned around to follow the imaginary line the dog was indicating.

Oh. There, behind him, was an immense gray building, suitable for your average mad scientist, or, considering its size, perhaps three or four mad scientists. What had the Plotmaster called it? The Citadel of Dread? Well, it was certainly well-named.

"Yip yip bark!" Dwight urged for emphasis.

So that was where Roger was supposed to go? He had to give Dwight credit. There was more than one way for a Wonder Dog to communicate.

"Okay, Dwight," Roger said aloud. "Let's get on with it." He frowned at the immense gray structure in front of them. From this angle, there didn't seem to be a window or other opening less than thirty feet from the ground. "But how do we get inside?"

"Yip!" Dwight replied as he bounced back and forth, tail wagging. "Arf, arf!"

"Do you know how to get in there?" Roger asked incredulously.

"Bark bark!" Dwight insisted. "Yip arf!"

"Okay, fella," Roger agreed with a laugh. "Lead on."

The Wonder Dog did as he was told, bounding ahead to circle the left-hand side of the citadel. Roger ran after him, following the dog into a depression that ran close to the giant structure's featureless wall—and it was quite a depression, too—as deep as Roger was tall.

That's when he heard it again. Music.

As soon as they were sheltered from the wind, Roger was once more aware of that orchestra that seemed to come from nowhere—and everywhere. Except, this time, the orchestra's music was even less pleasant than the time before. The horns and drums he had heard back on the Cop Movie world were gone, replaced by screeching violins.

Roger froze. He knew what happened in movies when you heard screeching violins.

Heard screeching violins? Music that came from nowhere—and everywhere?

Of course! That was where all this music was really coming from. He had been thinking too literally when he had looked around for a source to the sound back on that Cop Movie world. The music was behind them—and all around them—in the background! Every good movie had to have background music to heighten emotions and increase the tension. Why would the movie worlds of the Cineverse be any different? And he, since he had become Captain Crusader, had gained the ability to hear it!

He marveled again at his newfound power. No wonder that Captain Crusader was the hero's hero! When you could hear that anticipatory background music, you could be ready for anything!

Roger's elation, however, lasted only until he thought of the next, logical question:

What should you be ready for when you heard screeching violins?

Something nasty, was the first answer he came up with. Probably something deadly.

"Bark! Yip! Arf!"

Roger looked down at Dwight the Wonder Dog, who danced before him, eager to get on with it. Roger realized he had stopped for a moment, lost in thought. That was no way for the hero's hero to act, and it appeared to be Dwight's duty to tell him so. After all, if Roger thought about this in movie terms, the dog had become his sidekick now, and it was therefore Dwight's job to advance the action. There were certain Laws of the Cineverse, apparently, that would survive even the Change.

"Okay, fella!" Roger acknowledged. For now, he would choose to ignore those insistent violins. "Let's go!"

Dwight led the way again, out of the gully they had been traveling through—it actually looked rather like a half-completed moat—and around to the far side of the huge gray structure.

Roger grinned. This side was different. There, at the top of a mammoth staircase in the center of the immense building's huge wall, were two equally massive doors.

But, before Roger could even exclaim "Good boy!" he also realized that the doors came equipped with half a dozen incredibly burly guards, all sporting nasty-looking machine guns.

Roger felt something at his back. But not pressing into his back—no, it was more like somebody had grabbed his jogging jacket. That somebody pulled.

Roger was yanked off his feet. He fell on his back behind a low, dirt wall that led back to the gulley. Dwight stood above his head. The dog growled softly in his ear.

Roger looked back. The two of them were alone. That meant it had to have been Dwight, with his lightning-fast canine reflexes, who had grabbed Roger's jogging jacket and pulled him back to safety before the guards could spot him.

"What a Wonder Dog!" Roger whispered.

"Arf, bark," the dog replied humbly. He lifted himself onto his hind legs so that he could peer over the dirt wall. After a moment, apparently satisfied, he lowered himself back to all fours and looked at Roger.

"Bark! Yip yip!" Dwight chided softly.

"You're right," Roger agreed. "We have to be more careful." Wait a second. He had just responded to Dwight as if he'd actually understood the dog! But, then again, there had been a certain something about the canine's tone—

"But how can we get in there if we can't use the front door?"

Dwight put his nose to the ground, and began to sniff around their immediate surroundings, slowly wandering back down into the gulley.

After a moment, he made a small yelp of discovery. Dwight pawed at the dirt around whatever it was he had found. Roger got quickly to his feet and stepped forward to look over the dog's shoulder. There, set flush with the muddy ground, was a small, neatly lettered, white cardboard sign which read: SECRET TRAP DOOR RELEASE

The words were followed by an arrow. And, inches from the business end of that arrow, was a small, shiny brown knob.

"Should we?" Roger asked, still keeping his voice low.

"Bark!" Dwight insisted. He grabbed the knob between his mighty canine jaws and pulled.

There was a faint grinding noise somewhere beneath them, as if ancient machinery long disused had gone back into action.

Dwight barked softly as the ground fell away before them. The secret trapdoor had opened, forming a ramp that led below.

Roger followed the dog down into the darkness. The ramp sloped downward for maybe a dozen paces, then leveled off, Roger guessed, when they reached the true floor of the tunnel. It wasn't totally lightless down here, he realized. There was some dim illumination up ahead, an uneven light coming from what looked like a distant, sputtering torch.

Something boomed behind them. Roger spun around, but couldn't see anything beyond the dim tunnel. In fact, he could no longer see the ramp. The trapdoor had slammed shut behind them.

Slamming trap doors reminded him of nothing so much as haunted houses. He remembered before, when he had looked up at the fortress and thought of mad scientists. Could the Citadel of Dread be part of a Horror Movie world?

"Arf, bark yip!" Dwight called from up ahead. The dog must want Roger to follow him. And why not? Dwight hadn't steered him wrong yet.

And so they walked, down endless, featureless corridors, lit every hundred feet or so by what were indeed sputtering torches. At first, Roger was on his guard, expecting things to jump from side corridors or hidden passageways. But nothing did, and Dwight continued to trot on ahead, turning occasionally as, Roger guessed, his nose dictated, and—after a few minutes, or perhaps a few hours—Roger began to think of these corridors as *truly* endless. This was like a horror movie, too—a particularly bad one, which padded its few moments of plot with endless scenes of people traveling from place to place. Maybe, Roger thought, he should ask the Wonder Dog where they were going. That was, of course, if he could understand the canine's answer. Roger realized, for the first time since he had come to the Cineverse, he was actually getting a little bored. He wondered if this, too, was another aspect of the Change.

Then the music returned, more insistent than ever—and all violins. Violins went with horror movies, too, but they tended to swirl a lot in those films with ghosts and mad scientists. These violins, on the other hand, were definitely screeching, and Roger knew what kind of horror movies those kind of violins showed up in—the kind with knives and other sharp and unpleasant instruments of death.

Dwight whined softly. The dog knew something was wrong as well.

"What is it, boy?" Roger asked.

The dog growled deep in its throat.

"I don't understand."

Dwight replied with a series of short, staccato barks.

Roger could only shake his head. He was really stumped this time. "I still don't get it," he admitted. But, from the way the dog was acting, it had to be important.

The German shepherd stared at Roger for a long moment—almost as if he was considering how best to communicate. At long last, Dwight lifted a paw to tug at his ear.

"Ear?" Roger asked uncertainly. "Am I supposed to listen for something?"

Dwight shook his head and pawed at his ear again.

"Not supposed to hear? Something about sound?"

Dwight whined and kept on pawing. That meant Roger was getting close!

"Sound?" Roger asked as his mind searched wildly for meaning. "Sounds like?"

The Wonder Dog nodded rapidly as he barked in the affirmative.

Roger still didn't quite understand. "But sounds like what?"

Dwight hopped friskily back and forth.

"Move?" Roger ventured. "Hop? Jump?"

Dwight's pace became more agitated as he trotted back and forth along the width of the corridor.

"Fast? Speed? Run?"

Dwight stopped abruptly and nodded his sleek white head.

"Run?" Roger clapped his hands. He had gotten it at last! "Sounds like run? Ton? Fun? Bun?"

Dwight sat there and watched him. Roger hadn't guessed it yet.

"Sun?" he tried. "Gun?"

Dwight leapt up and down, silently but with great animation.

"Gun?" Roger said, more to himself than to the dog. "Somebody's got a gun?" That could go a long way towards explaining the violins.

Dwight lifted a paw in front of his muzzle, the closest a dog could get, Roger realized, to making a shusshing sound. Roger stopped talking, and listened.

There was another sound in the distance—a voice, repeating a single word, over and over, a word that he couldn't quite hear over the music. But that voice was getting closer, and louder, as the violins built to a screaming crescendo. Then, as quickly as the music had begun, it was over.

Roger could hear that word clearly now, for the voice

sounded as if it was very close. It was indeed saying a single word—and that word wasn't one Roger particularly looked forward to hearing.

"Obliterate," was all the voice said. "Obliterate."

17

It took far too long to select the bunnies.

Louie realized he had made a mistake as soon as he asked Fluffytail to help him choose—and Fluffytail's idea of decision-making was to let every bunny speak in turn. Spottynose thought only the bunnies with the most colorful markings should go. Highjumper, on the other hand, thought only the bunnies with the best leaping ability should be sent. Pointy-ears, however, remarked that bunnies should be chosen on the basis of unique personal traits. And Largebottom, well—it hurt Louie's brain to even think about all the different bunny arguments, especially since, when they fought, they did it with those ridiculously high bunny voices.

And the arguments went nowhere. The Change would be over, the Cineverse destroyed, and the bunnies would be discussing whether they should choose on the basis of tails or paws.

Louie had had enough. He had lost control. He had yelled at them. He had told them to shut up. He had further told them he never wanted to hear another bunny argument as long as he lived.

He had immediately been confronted by the most profound silence he had ever heard—a silence intensified by a hundred pairs of incredibly cute—and incredibly hurt—bunny eyes, all two hundred of them boring straight into his soul.

"Uh, er—" Louie had replied. "Um, uh—" But no words came to mind, for what words could combat *that*? Louie had never felt this awful before, even in his brief career as a villain. It was only then that he truly realized what a powerful weapon he had at his disposal. Cute bunnies might have been a formidable foe—but *hurt*, cute bunnies would be virtually unstoppable.

"Zabana cannot face this!" the jungle prince cried, echoing Louie's sentiments.

"Dang straight!" Doc wailed. "Choose these varmints, or, pledge or no pledge, I'm goin' back to the bottle!"

So Louie chose quickly, before all those eyes could overwhelm him again. He picked Bouncer for obvious reasons, Fluffytail for his leadership capabilities, and Highjumper because he was the only bunny whose argument had made any sense. After that, he had picked the next four bunnies to Highjumper's left. Seven seemed like a lucky number. Besides, any more bunnies (especially considering the size of Bouncer) and Louie would be afraid of straining the limits of his Captain Crusader Decoder Ring.

He turned away quickly from all the bunnies that would have to be left behind. He knew, without even looking, that bunny eyes, disappointed bunny eyes, not as bad as hurt bunny eyes, but still bad enough, would be more than his sidekick heart could bear.

But now it was time to leave, and face the might of Doctor Dread! He marched back toward the dark tunnel where they had entered Bunnyland, waving his fellows and the chosen bunnies to follow.

"Mother of mercy!" Officer O'Clanrahan muttered as he joined Louie's rapid march. "I'm glad that's over!"

In a way, Louie was surprised that the cop even knew what was going on. The officer had certainly kept his distance from the bunnies—in fact, lately he seemed to be keeping his distance from everyone. Without Dwight the Wonder Dog around, the policeman seemed to be disintegrating before Louie's eyes, the once-proud officer always hanging back and muttering to himself. In all his years as a sidekick, Louie didn't think he had ever seen such a change.

But perhaps "change" was the key word to everything in the Cineverse. Maybe the Change didn't just affect movie worlds. Maybe it affected individuals as well.

That thought was not comforting in the least. If O'Clanrahan was changing, perhaps all of them were changing as well, in ways they couldn't imagine—or worse, ways they might not even notice. Louie had spent great amounts of energy trying to rid himself of his role in sidekick comedy relief. But what now, if his own personality changed without him even knowing it? He shivered.

"But—" one of the bunnies yelled out from the pack that he had left behind, "you can't leave yet!"

Oh, no. Louie might be frightened now, but if he had to take one more look at those bunny eyes, he might become downright suicidal.

"That's right!" Louie cringed as another bunny called out: "We need to send you off with a happy bunny song!"

Somewhere nearby, a very happy orchestra began to play as scores of rabbits lifted their high soprano voices in song:

"We've got the grass and the sky of blue,
We've got flowers and carrots, too.
Life with bunnies is so profound.
There's always more bunnies to go around!"

"That's the spirit!" Fluffytail called back from close by Louie's side. "Second verse!"

The massed bunnydom answered in song:

"Days grow short and time just flies,
But with bunnies your cheer just multiplies!
Every time you look out there in the sun,
There's always more bunnies having fun!"

Louie had to admit, now that he thought of it, that there could be worse ways of marching to battle than with a cheerful song at your back. Heck, he'd even forgotten whatever it was he'd been worrying about a moment ago. With bunnies on his side, how could he help but win?

They had once again reached the entrance to the cave. Louie boldly strode forward into the darkness.

"Yay, bunnies!" Bouncer's loud but none-too-bright voice echoed around him. "Verse number three!"

"We bunnies like to stick around,
We'll even follow you underground!
We can hop at all different speeds,
There's always more bunnies to meet your needs!"

"Halt!" Zabana said from somewhere just ahead. "We have reached the Pit!"

Louie squinted. Not having Zabana's jungle-trained senses, he couldn't see much of anything. He looked aloft, and saw a distant circle of light, the upper entrance to the Pit, a hundred yards and more above them.

"Is ladder here," the jungle prince explained from somewhere in the nearby gloom. "Can climb back up!"

"Faith and begorrah!" Officer O'Clanrahan moaned. "It'll take us forever to climb up there!"

"Not if you have bunnies to help you along!" one of the the nearby rabbits said cheerily.

Louie felt a strong hand grab his wrist.

"Here," Zabana explained. "Ladder in front of you."

With Zabana's guidance, Louie reached forward, and indeed did feel a wooden rung of what must be the ladder that reached all the way to the top of the Pit.

"You leader," Zabana added. "You go first."

Yes, Louie guessed he was the leader, and he'd better lead. He felt around with his foot until he found a lower rung, then pushed himself up the ladder.

"Doc, you next. Then O'Clanrahan. Zabana help bunnies."

"Bouncer help bunnies, too!"

Louie pulled himself up slowly, feeling his way up the ladder a couple of rungs at a time. He was glad some of the others were taking turns giving orders—it was somehow reassuring to the sidekick in his soul.

"They're on their way!" a rabbit voice called from down below. "Fourth verse, guys!"

And the bunny chorus replied:

"Oh, bunnies are the loving sort,
We can play and we cavort.
'Til we're once again in the family way;
There's always more bunnies to save the day!"

At least, Louie thought, the song gave him a little additional rhythm with which to climb. In fact, it seemed to be getting lighter already. He could see the ladder in front of him now—quite clearly, actually. They must be making some progress.

"Whoo-ee!" Doc whistled from just beneath. "Look where we've gotten to."

"Hey, guys!" The bunny voice seemed incredibly distant. "Is it time for the fifth verse?"

Louie looked up. That tiny point of light he had seen above them was now a great blue circle in the sky. They were almost there!

"Why," he muttered aloud, "we're almost to the top!"

"Never seen its like," Doc agreed from just below, "in all my years as an animal trainer." He spat in the darkness. "Not to mention the time I put in as a high-wire trapeze artist."

So, movie magic had worked again, and the bunny song had shortened their climb considerably. Louie had to admit it: despite the danger of the Change, there were certain advantages to having your adventure in a place like the Cineverse. Faintly, he heard the bunnies begin verse number five:

"We like to hop and we like to jump,
When we're in the dark bunnies like to—"

"Who challenges me from the Pit of Absurdity?" a woman's voice shouted, drowning out the distant song.

Now that they had left the rabbits behind, they would once again have to face Hippolita and her boys. Louie took a deep breath and pulled himself up the final rung of the ladder so that he could see over the lip of the Pit.

But it wasn't Hippolita who glowered at him. It was a somewhat older woman, with blond hair and a whip. Still, there was something very familiar about her, despite her black leather costume—Wasn't she Roger's mother?

"Who dares to stare at Mother Antoinette?" she demanded. The whip danced in her hand.

"Oh," another, only slightly less forceful female voice interjected. "Not you again."

It was Bertha—his sister. And next to her stood Menge the Merciless and Professor Peril. Big Louie had climbed into a den of evil!

"So, pardner!" Doc called from down below. "What's holding things up?"

"Uh—" Louie replied as tactfully as he could. "We've got some problem—"

"How dare you not answer me, worm?" Mother Antoinette's voice cut him off mid-word.

"Um—" Louie's head snapped back up. He had forgotten all about the woman with the whip. Who should he talk to first? Sidekicks shouldn't have to make these sorts of decisions!

The whip snaked around his neck, pulling him from the top of the ladder and throwing him onto the ground a half-dozen feet from the pit. Louie grabbed at the leather. He couldn't breathe.

"And you claim to know this toad?" Mother Antoinette asked Bertha.

"I'm afraid so," Bertha admitted. "I'm afraid he's my brother."

"But he's on the other side!" Menge added helpfully.

"No mercy," Professor Peril added succinctly, "not even for relatives!"

Mother Antoinette smiled grimly. "You forget who my son is." She jerked her hand back, and the whip left Louie's neck. "No mercy, *especially* for relatives!"

Louie massaged his neck as he gasped for air. He had gotten his fellows into this mess. How could he get them out of it?

"Now hold on a second there, little lady," Doc drawled from where he now stood at the edge of the Pit. "That's no way to talk about kin."

Mother Antoinette flicked her wrist.

CRACK the whip snapped in the air. *CRACK* *CRACK* *CRACK*

Doc glanced distractedly down at the twin pearl-handled revolvers in his gun belt. "These danged things won't work in these here parts, will they?"

Mother Antoinette allowed herself a small smile.

"A whip works anywhere."

Louie's hand involuntarily returned to his neck. He'd had enough of being a hero.

Where was Captain Crusader when you really needed him?

18

Obliterate?

That's what this stranger was saying. Not only that, but according to Dwight's sign language, this guy had a gun. And the Plotmaster hadn't given Roger any kind of a weapon at all! Roger was totally unarmed, except, perhaps, for his wits.

"Bark!" Dwight remarked reassuringly. "Arf! Bark!"

"Oblit—" The nearby voice paused in its destructive chant. "Was that a dog?"

Uh-oh. Dwight had made a tactical error. The Wonder Dog wagged his tail a bit sheepishly.

"Well," the ever-nearer voice asserted, "I can obliterate a dog, too! Here, poochy poochy!"

Dwight looked at Roger in disbelief, and Roger had to agree. Poochy poochy?

"There you are!" The owner of the voice, a man in a guard's uniform festooned with medals, stepped out of an intersecting corridor, and quickly drew his gun.

Dwight the Wonder Dog was faster. He leapt forward with a speed and ferocity that Roger hadn't seen before, as if the canine had a special vendetta against this guard. And, Roger realized, perhaps he did. Perhaps anyone who called Dwight the Wonder Dog "poochy poochy" would have faced such retribution.

The guard didn't stand a chance against the animal's superior reflexes. Dwight bowled the human over, and the gun went flying as the dog's momentum carried him over the fallen guard to bounce against the wall beyond.

"Stop where you are!" Roger instructed as the guard struggled to get up and retrieve his gun. "We've got you outnumbered!'' He whistled to the dog. ''C'mon, Dwight. Let's round up our prisoner and see if we can get him to talk!''

But Dwight didn't move. He sat in the spot where he had bounced, and looked quizzically at Roger. ''Yip?''

Something was wrong. ''Dwight, fella!'' Roger called. ''What's the matter?''

The Wonder Dog looked at the wall, then back at Roger. ''Yip?''

Oh, no. Dwight wasn't responding well at all. Roger realized the dog must have bounced off the wall headfirst.

The guard saw that something was wrong, too. He jumped for his gun, and he got it.

''Yip?'' Dwight remarked.

''Now the tables have turned,'' the guard announced with a grin as he once again brandished his weapon, a nasty, futuristic-looking revolver. ''Doctor Dread did not make me Captain of the Guard for nothing! Now, I can obliterate you trespassing scum at my leisure.''

''Yip?'' Dwight interjected.

''That's correct,'' the Captain of the Guard continued, as if answering the dog's question. ''It is my job—and I take pleasure in doing it—to destroy any and all who have the temerity to enter Doctor Dread's domain unauthorized! You should take this last moment to dwell on the suicidal foolishness of your plans, before I pull the trigger on my Obliteration Ray and blow a hole in your midsection the size of a cannonball!''

''Uh—'' Roger couldn't help himself. ''Excuse me?''

The Captain of the Guard looked up from aiming his Obliteration Ray. ''Yes?''

''Do you always talk at such length before blowing people away?''

The Captain reddened slightly. ''Well, I have so few chances—I mean, villains are supposed to—'' He cleared his throat. ''Look, it's a failing of mine, all right?'' He once again lifted and aimed his weapon. ''Now. Do you have any final words before your guts are splattered all over this underground passageway?''

This, Roger realized, was the real (and perhaps final) opportunity for him to use his wits, as Roger or as Captain Crusader. But what could he say upon meeting a potential assassin? There was only time to repeat the first thing that came into Roger's head:

''First impressions are always the most important.''

The look of anger on the guard's face was replaced by an odd little smile. ''If you say so—'' he began pleasantly, but then shook his head violently. ''No! You may be disguised in that dirty blue jogging suit, but I know who you are! You're Captain Crusader!''

Roger shrugged his shoulders. Were his sayings getting that obvious? Maybe he was doing something right.

''You won't fool me with those Captain Crusader expressions!'' The guard clicked the safety off his nasty looking weapon. ''My job is to obliterate you, and obliterate you I shall!''

Uh-oh. It was time for Roger to say something else.

''You may erase the answer,'' he replied, ''but the problem still remains.''

''Really?'' the guard remarked, open-mouthed. He seemed to have forgotten all about the gun. ''There's something about that that's almost—profound.'' He shook his head. ''No! I won't be swayed by aphorisms! It's death for you, Captain Crusader!'' But this time, when he aimed the Obliteration Ray, his hand was shaking. Roger could feel the situation turn to his advantage.

''Yip?'' Dwight remarked uncertainly. And there, Roger thought, was his next saying.

''Death may come and death may go,'' Roger said loudly, ''but a dog is a buddy for life!''

''Really?'' The Captain of the Guards seemed to be blinking back tears. ''That's beautiful!'' His gun hand dropped again. ''How can I shoot somebody who says things like that?''

It was time for Roger to deliver the one-two punch.

Maybe a new variation of something tried-and-true would do to start.

"Killing Captain Crusader," Roger announced, "is like a day without sunshine."

"How true!" The Captain of the Guard's frown was twisting into a rapturous smile. Still, Roger didn't feel it was time to stop, yet. He needed a final saying for the capper. This time, the words flowed from his tongue:

"A bad deed is like a piece of manure, rotting in the darkness, but a good deed grows like a flower!"

"Wow!" The guardsman tossed his gun to the ground. "I give up! I can't help it. I'm on your side now."

"Really?" Roger replied, then realized that might not be the best answer for someone who was supposed to be as decisive as Captain Crusader. "Really!" he exclaimed, turning his question into a positive exclamation. "Captain Crusader is everybody's friend!"

The guardsman nodded eagerly. "That's the positive attitude I like to hear! Now that I'm working for Captain Crusader, what could possibly go wrong?"

"Yip?" Dwight answered.

The Wonder Dog was still not himself. When Dwight rammed his head against the wall, he seemed to have lost something. Roger wondered if dogs could get amnesia.

"Yip?" Dwight repeated. He looked back at the wall, as if, perhaps, he had left his memory there when he bounced.

Roger couldn't stand to see the Wonder Dog in such a state. There had to be something—There *was* something he could do! Surely if Captain Crusader could get one of Doctor Dread's minions to see the light, he should be able to help a stunned Wonder Canine.

"Dwight?" he called.

"Yip?" the dog replied. At least, Roger thought it was a reply. The dog was still staring at the wall.

"Listen, Dwight," he insisted. But what should he say? Perhaps he should tailor this particular saying to canine interests. It certainly couldn't hurt. Still, with Dwight's current mental condition, he wanted to keep it simple.

"A police dog is your friend," Roger tried.

"Yip?" Dwight answered.

That was it, huh? Maybe, Roger thought, he had kept it too simple. These Captain Crusader adages had started to come all too easily to him. Perhaps, for these things to really work, Captain Crusader had to break a bit of a mental sweat.

"Okay, Dwight," he instructed the dog, who had turned back to look at Roger. "It's important to listen to this one."

"Yip?" At least the dog was answering, in his limited way. Roger was encouraged to try one more time. And this one had to be good. But what did *dogs* consider good? A clean food dish is a happy food dish? Still too simple. But perhaps food would make a proper subject matter.

"A bone in the mouth is good for today," Roger said, slowly yet clearly, "but a bone buried in the yard is forever."

Dwight stared at him for a long moment.

"Yip?" the dog said at last.

"I thought that one was pretty good," the Captain of the Guard interjected.

Roger nodded grimly. He knew it was the best he could do. But, now that he really looked at the dog's vacant stare, he was afraid it wasn't only him. There was a real communication problem here. Ever since he'd bumped his head, Dwight just didn't seem to get it anymore. How could he cure the dog if the dog couldn't understand him? There were limits to Captain Crusader's power after all.

"So," the Captain of the Guard ventured, "what do we do now, Captain Crusader?"

He glanced over at the eager guardsman. That question sounded suspiciously like another example of moving the plot along. With Dwight out of commission, would the Captain of the Guard take over the sidekick role? The mysterious ways of the Cineverse were truly staggering.

But the guard, sidekick or no, required an answer. Was this former minion of Doctor Dread really on Roger's side now? Roger remembered a time not so long ago, when he had asked himself the same question about Big Louie, a sidekick who had turned out to be one of his staunchest allies.

Roger decided it was worth giving a shot. What else would one expect of Captain Crusader?

"We must continue to the very heart of the Citadel of Dread," he replied, "so that we can capture Doctor Dread and put an end to his evil."

"Gee," the guard replied as his smile returned. "You mean good guys can talk like that, too? Maybe this change of heart won't be so bad after all."

The smile vanished from the guardsman's lips as he stared off into the distance. As the Captain spoke, Roger noticed the music was back, with a full orchestra welling up behind him.

"Still," the guardsman began solemnly, "it won't be easy. This place is not called the Citadel of Dread for nothing. There'll be scores of heavily armed men, many of them as ruthless as I was only a moment ago. And there won't be only simple weapons like my Obliteration Ray to contend with—no, there'll be superscientific marvels like the Zeta Ray and the Buchanan Device to contend with, all controlled by the most diabolical of Dread's henchpeople. And I haven't even mentioned the booby traps filled with wild animals and poisoned spikes and impossibly large boulders crashing out of nowhere! The citadel is the sort of place where most people are doomed before they start. And what can the two of us"—he glanced distractedly at the spacey Wonder Dog—"or even three, do against all that might?"

Doomed before they started? That certainly sounded like a good description of their present situation to Roger. He had no idea the Citadel of Dread was so formidable.

"But what am I talking about? Of course!" The Captain of the Guard laughed at his own foolishness. "I forgot! You're Captain Crusader! This should be no problem at all."

Well, Roger thought, at least somebody had confidence

in him. Maybe another function of the sidekick was to make the hero feel more heroic. Why, then, wasn't it working for him?

Still, what other options did he have? Now that Captain Crusader was here, he had to see this through to the end. There was nothing else for Roger to do but follow the guardsman deeper into the citadel.

"Yip?" Dwight remarked as he trotted after them.

19

"Curse you, Mother Antoinette!" another woman's voice shouted.

Louie looked beyond the woman with the whip, and saw Hippolita and her three muscular cohorts all handily tied to nearby trees. Louie wondered for an instant where Dread's gang had gotten the rope. Still, as an experienced sidekick, he knew that when the plot demanded something, that something always seemed to show up.

"Now the tide will turn!" the son of Samson added. Louie noticed the muscleman hadn't gotten any better at getting his lip movement to match his words. "Our champions have returned!"

Mother Antoinette regarded Louie and his fellows—who were, one by one, crawling from the pit—with a visible sneer. "So these are your so-called—" she hesitated in a manner worthy of Doctor Dread—"champions?"

"Well," Hippolita admitted as Officer O'Clanrahan and then Zabana emerged from the darkness, "you have to take what you're given. Consider the raw materials."

This did not appease Mother Antoinette in the least. "And you dare compare them to me?" This time, her whip danced in the direction of her captives.

CRACK *CRACK* *CRACK*

"No!" the second cousin of Goliath groveled. "We swear! *You* can be Born out of rock!"

"Before this is all over," Mother Antoinette agreed, "I'll be born out of rock and more! Now, pardon me while I—deal with these interlopers!"

"Before you harm fluffy hair on bunnies' head," a jungle-trained voice interjected, "you deal with Zabana first!"

"Bunnies?" Professor Peril interjected, cutting to the core. "Yes, they've brought the bunnies with them! Then we *are* in the right place after all."

"First things first, Prince of the Jungle," Doc drawled as he casually walked toward Mother Antoinette. "Me and this little lady have some talkin' to do."

Doc's remarks didn't appear to make Mother Antoinette any happier.

"You don't deserve talk," she murmured, her teeth clenched in anger. "You deserve the whip!"

CRACK *CRACK* *CRACK*

She whirled her weapon above her head for effect before she attacked.

"Well," Doc replied easily, "if that's the way you want it."

Louie flinched as the whip lashed out toward Doc's midsection. But, when the whip arrived, Doc was no longer there.

CRACK

Doc somersaulted quickly and landed back on his feet. Mother Antoinette was undeterred. She flicked her wrist, and her leather thong of destruction changed course, flashing for Doc's neck.

Doc reacted every bit as quickly, falling away from the lash as he kicked his right foot high, so that the leather tip was deflected harmlessly off the heel of his boot.

CRACK *CRACK*

Mother Antoinette screamed in frustration, whirling the whip once again above her head.

CRACK *CRACK* *CRACK*

With a low growl, she threw the business end of the whip forward one more time, straight at Doc's face!

This time, though, the Westerner simply sidestepped the deadly leather, and, once the whip had snapped harmlessly in the air a foot from his ear, he grabbed the whip end before it could *CRACK* again.

Doc yanked.

The mistress of the whip cried out in surprise. While she

somehow managed to hold on to her weapon, Doc's sudden move pulled her out of her incredibly high heels and onto the ground.

"There, missy," Doc remarked, his face set in the kind of grim expression that showed he didn't particularly enjoy this sort of business. "I didn't mean to be rough, but, sometimes, a man's gotta do what a man's gotta do."

Mother Antoinette's only answer was a deep-throated growl as she struggled to get up. Louie had a feeling this wasn't over yet.

"Just a little something I picked up in my years studying the Oriental arts," Doc continued self-deprecatingly while keeping a firm grip on his end of the whip. "Amazing what you could learn from those folks workin' on the railroad."

"Ha-ha!" Hippolita called from her tree. "Laugh at our champions now! They have returned with the Jewel of the Seven Cities, and we will be undefeatable!"

The Jewel of the Seven Cities? Louie frowned. Oh, yeah, there had been some mention about that in all the gobbledygook Hippolita and her boys had spouted before they had thrown them into the Pit. With all the business about the dark cave and the bunnies and all, Louie had forgotten completely about the jewel.

"Jewel? You mean this jewel?" Bouncer asked, pointing to the ostentatiously large ruby in his navel.

Why hadn't Louie seen that jewel there before? Could it have been hidden under the fluffy bunny fur or—oh—of course—it *had* to be hidden—something, Louie reminded himself, to do with the plot. When he had been a simple sidekick, he wouldn't have even thought to question that sort of thing. Now that he was trying to lead people, he had to get control of things, and, when you tried to get control of things in the Cineverse—

Professor Peril whistled as he stared at Bouncer. "I haven't seen this guy before. That's a bunny?"

"Not just any bunny," muttered Bertha, who, Louie recalled, had had business with Bouncer before. "You've got to watch out for his exploding carrots. I imagine Doctor

Dread would not be—displeased if this was the first bunny we obliterated."

Bouncer hopped over to Louie, all six-feet-plus, two hundred pounds of solid bunny muscle bouncing across the landscape. It was a disquieting sight, even for someone who was the large rabbit's ally.

"Want to see Bouncer's jewel?" The rabbit popped the large ruby out of his navel before Louie had a chance to answer. Bouncer tossed it into Louie's hands, and the sometime sidekick saw that it had a felt tag attached, a tag with a neatly lettered label that read:

THE JEWEL OF THE SEVEN CITIES
CERTIFICATE OF AUTHENTICITY
DO NOT REMOVE UNDER PENALTY OF LAW

"Very nice," Louie murmured, handing the jewel back to Bouncer. But what did it all mean?

"We must have that jewel!" Hippolita declared in her usual out-of-sync fashion. "Bring it here, or face the wrath of the Oracle of Venus!"

But Mother Antoinette had regained both her feet and her high heels. "If you take that jewel anywhere, you'll face the wrath of something a lot closer than Venus!" She pulled the whip away from a startled Doc, who spun about with the force of her tug.

CRACK

Doc ducked, barely avoiding the whip as he rolled again. But this time Mother Antoinette was ready for him.

CRACK *CRACK*

The whip snapped to either side of Doc, forcing him into a hasty somersault. Even then, the Westerner could not escape.

CRACK *CRACK* *CRACK*

Doc pivoted, then executed a handstand followed by a

slightly clumsy backflip. The whip still caught him, wrapping itself around his boot.

Doc fell flat on his back and moved no more. Mother Antoinette paused to smile evilly.

"Doc!" Louie called. "Are you all right?"

Doc raised his head and blinked groggily. "I'll be jusht fine, shoon ash I getsh my breath."

Oh, no! The reformed town drunk was inebriated once again, this time from the extreme dizziness brought on by his narrow escapes!

But—Louie realized—this was terrible! Who besides Doc could stand up to the prowess of Mother Antoinette?

Apparently, Mother Antoinette had the same idea. She paused a further moment to grin conspiratorially at her cohorts before issuing her ultimatum:

"Surrender, or face the wrath of Mother—" She stopped as she saw the uncertain expressions on the faces of her companions. "I mean, the wrath of Doctor Dread."

For some reason, that change of phrase seemed to make her company a touch more relaxed. Louie wondered it there was some discord in the ranks of Doctor Dread. Perhaps, he considered, there might be more than one way to defeat the ultimate master of evil.

"Zabana fight jungle snake!" the Prince of the Jungle declared. "Zabana fight whip, too!"

"Fools!" Hippolita called from within her ropes. "You must use the jewel to be truly free!"

"Bouncer likes jewel," the very large rabbit admitted as he leaned forward to admire his navel ornament. "But what does jewel do?"

"It is simplicity itself!" Hippolita explained, "all you have to—"

CRACK Mother Antoinette's whip interrupted the explanation.

"I will not be silenced!" Hippolita exclaimed. "The secret might of Sparta is hidden—"

CRACK *CRACK* The whip stripped bark from the tree close by Hippolita's left ear, then her right.

"The sixth labor of Hercules—" Hippolita tried again.

CRACK went the whip between her legs.

"The secret of the Golden Fleece—" Hippolita added hastily.

CRACK snapped the whip as it sliced through a half-dozen strands of her strikingly blond hair.

"Er—" Hippolita blurted as she gulped down her fear, "remember the Trojan Horse—"

CRACK The whip curled itself around the rope securing Hippolita's shoulders to the tree. Antoinette tugged once, and the rope moved upward, until it was pressing into Hippolita's neck!

"Perhaps—" Hippolita gasped, "I will be silenced—after all."

"You will say nothing more," Mother Antoinette declared with grim satisfaction, "until the rest of these scum have surrendered." She turned her less than pleasant grin on Louie. "If you do not surrender, you will see your fellows humiliated, and more. And—once we are done with them—we will begin on you."

"Right," Louie replied, indicating that he understood, but not that he agreed.

"Shurrender?" Doc shouted from his still-horizontal vantage point. " It'sh the lasht thing we'll do!"

"Never!" Zabana agreed. "Zabana not know meaning of word surrender!"

"Bouncer has vocabulary problems, too," the large rabbit admitted. "That's why Zabana is Bouncer's friend. But what should Bouncer do with jewel?"

The rabbits whispered among themselves that they were far too cute to surrender. Even Officer O'Clanrahan seemed to have swallowed his misgivings enough to be grimly silent. So Louie surmised, they were all in agreement on that at least—no surrender.

"Not surrender, no," Louie stated his decision aloud, as he thought that that decision left them with only two courses of action. Now, he had to guess as to the results of those actions. He looked over at the four tied to the trees. As nasty as Mother Antoinette appeared, Louie didn't think she'd simply murder these local characters for the fun of it. In fact, Hippolita and her musclemen would probably be far safer if Mother Antoinette was no longer tempted to use them as a bargaining device.

A hero would lead the others forward, oblivious to danger, until the prisoners were freed, or he and his fellows were killed or captured. Under normal circumstances, the hero would win, too.

But, one look at his surroundings showed Louie these circumstances were anything but normal. Musclemen, bunnies, Mother Antoinette—the Change was in full swing now. And, Louie knew from past experience, whenever they were in the midst of the Change, the wrong things happened. Heroes died, villains won, things ended unhappily. And, looking at the way Mother Antoinette had the upper hand, that sort of ending seemed not only likely but almost inevitable.

If Louie were really a hero, they'd still have to stay here and fight. But whoever said he was a hero? Seeing as he was really a sidekick, he couldn't think of a single thing wrong with the other course of action open to them—running.

"Come on, folks!" he yelled to the others. "We're not surrendering! We're getting out of here!"

His fellows gathered quickly around him. Louie twisted the Captain Crusader Ring on his finger, carefully shielding his movements from prying eyes. If the villains couldn't see his setting, they wouldn't be able to follow him. And, if they could get to Doctor Dread's hideout first, perhaps they could deal with the ultimate master of evil without his minions being anywhere around.

Mother Antoinette and her fellow felons gaped at them as Louie completed their escape.

"See you in the funny papers!" Louie almost laughed as the blue smoke rose around them, freeing them from a potentially deadly situation.

But how could he laugh when he knew—even though he'd had no time to tell his fellows—that the place he was using the Captain Crusader Decoder Ring to take them might be even worse?

20

"Stop right here!" the Captain of the Guard commanded.

Roger stopped. The last couple of times the Captain had issued this sort of warning, they had barely missed being decapitated by rotating sawblades and being skewered by six-foot-long iron spikes. The Captain had explained this was the sort of thing one had to expect in the citadel, especially when one took the seldom used subbasement route.

This time, though, there were no noisy blades or messy spikes. In fact, Roger couldn't see anything at all.

"False alarm?" he asked the Captain quietly.

"Anything but." The Captain pointed to the floor of the hallway a half-dozen feet ahead. At first Roger didn't see a thing in the dim and inconsistent light, and then he thought his eyes were playing tricks on him. The gray floor was moving, rolling and shifting around as if it were a liquid rather than a solid. But whatever that glistening, ever-changing surface was, it appeared to be alive.

"Killer flatworms," the guard replied to the question Roger was about to ask.

"Killer *flatworms*?" Roger asked incredulously.

The Captain nodded, his gaze drawn back to the wriggling mass. "It's their bite, I think. Or maybe they have poisonous spikes or something. Doctor Dread wasn't too precise about the specifics."

Roger shivered. "He never is, is he?"

"You've noticed that too? Whatever, those worms are deadly. It's one of the subtler forms of death hereabouts—although I do understand it's incredibly lingering and painful." The Captain shrugged. "It's amazing the variations you can get on death and destruction when you have all of the Cineverse at your disposal."

Roger shivered a second time. He didn't think killer flatworms would care in the least if he was Roger Gordon or Captain Crusader or anybody else for that matter. Thank goodness—or perhaps the Plotmaster—that he had managed to gain a guide through this deadly place.

He glanced at the guard. "You generally don't stumble around here in the dark, do you?"

"Only in daytime, if you can help it," the Captain agreed.

Roger watched the swirling movement of the worms—rather hypnotic, in its way. He shook himself. There was a question he felt he had to ask. "But what happens if you have to, well, you know—"

The Captain instantly understood his meaning. "It's amazing what incentive will do to let you hold things in till morning."

"Yip?" Dwight added, as if this were a concept that even the addled Wonder Dog might understand.

Roger had another question. "So how do we get out of this one?"

"Hold on a second," the guard replied. "It's around here somewhere." He looked toward the ceiling and pointed. "Ah."

Roger looked up to where the Captain indicated. There, somewhat hidden by the rusted pipes and dusty air ducts, but plainly visible once you knew where to look, was a neatly lettered cardboard sign:

WORM-CONTROL LEVER
PULL FOR RELEASE

The Captain of the Guard reached up on tiptoe until his hand closed over the dust-covered lever. He pulled it down. There was the all-too familiar grinding of seldom used machinery. And something slid open beneath the worms.

The worms hissed as they fell into the pit. Before this, Roger hadn't known worms made any sound at all. It was probably a hidden talent of killer flatworms, he reflected.

The steel door slid shut again, now devoid of the deadly crawlers.

"Wow," Roger admitted. "I never realized that getting to Doctor Dread would be this difficult."

"We do have to take the most disused and forsaken passageways within the citadel, so that we will escape detection by the forces of Doctor Dread," the Captain of the Guard summarized neatly. "Even I, however, am amazed how disused and forsaken some of these passageways are."

Uh-oh, Roger thought. He was forgetting where he was, and who he was. Captain Crusader should always be positive, especially when something as potentially deadly as the Change was taking place. Roger remembered when he had been facing the Cowabungamunga, and how he had almost fallen before the mightiest of surfing waves when he had doubted his ability, but had regained his prowess the minute he had begun to sing a positive surfing song.

Something similar could be happening here at this very moment. The way to Dread's inner sanctum was proving to be long and arduous. Roger was losing heart despite himself, and it seemed that his newfound guide was losing faith as well—and Roger wasn't sure how strong the Captain of the Guard's faith was in the first place. It was time for Captain Crusader to do something about it. Somehow, singing seemed inappropriate in a place as bleak as this. Captain Crusader's other ability, however, could be used anywhere.

"The road may be long and weary," he said in a loud, firm voice, "but justice waits for us at the end."

"I'm glad you said that," the Captain of the Guard said with a relieved smile. "Why was I hesitating? Let's go get them!"

The Captain of the Guard strode boldly forward across the spot so recently covered by killer worms. Roger followed, and wished he could be that confident. The more time he spent in the Cineverse, however, the more he realized he might be the only thing preventing the Change from taking over everything!

"I think we're getting closer," the guard called over his shoulder. "It's been a long time since I've been down here, but we can't be more than a half an hour from the hidden panel."

But Roger's last aphorism had given him an idea. He remembered the Cowabungamunga once again, and how, every time he sang another verse of a surfing song, he would magically find himself farther along in his race against the killer wave. It seemed that Captain Crusader homilies worked on much the same principle as those songs—it was all movie magic, after all—but would that principle hold up in a place like the Citadel of Dread?

Well, it was worth a Captain Crusader try.

He looked about at his truly dingy surroundings.

"On the other side of the thickest wall," he said, "the sun is shining bright."

The guard stopped at the intersection to two seemingly identical corridors. "You know, we may be closer than I thought."

Well, perhaps that was just chance—or perhaps his powers of aphorism were working again. Roger decided a repeat performance couldn't hurt.

"A caged bird still can sing," Roger commented.

"Yes!" the guard cheered. "I'm sure that secret panel is around here somewhere!"

He frowned at his surroundings. Perhaps, Roger considered, he needed more encouragement.

"Uh," Roger added hurriedly, "a caged hamster can still run on his wheel."

"I think it's over on this wall—" the guard mused.

"And—um—" Roger added quickly, not wanting to lose the momentum, "—a caged lion gets fed on a regular basis."

"But I can't remember where it is, exactly," the Captain added with a frown.

Roger had to admit that the guard might have gotten stalled on account of him. It was possible that Captain Crusader had overmined that particular metaphor. You needed more than a positive attitude in this business—you needed originality.

"Um—er—" Roger tried again. Still, it was tough to think of anything original—or more specifically, original and uplifting—in a place as dingy and depressing as this. But Roger had to try. He looked up at the slimy green walls.

"Mold may be disgusting," he ventured, "but it still needs a mother's love."

"I've found it!" the Captain of the Guard exulted. "Now, if only I can determine how it opens."

Roger walked over behind the guard. "Look up," he suggested.

The guard looked, and saw the cardboard sign with its neatly printed instructions.

SECRET PASSAGEWAY
TO DREAD'S INNER SANCTUM
PRESS WALL IMMEDIATELY BELOW.

The instructions were followed by another helpful arrow.

The Captain of the Guard pressed. The wall slid aside. It was dark on the other side. The Captain of the Guard stepped through first. Roger followed.

"Yip?" Dwight commented at Roger's heels.

"Yes, fella," Roger murmured as he patted Dwight's head. He had hoped that once he had gotten a little time and distance from his actions the Wonder Dog might snap out of his funk, but apparently it wasn't going to happen. Roger hated to see the once-vital hound like this, and he swore, once he had dealt with the Change and found Delores, the next thing he would concentrate on would be a cure for Dwight.

Ahead, Roger saw the guard's dim shadow reach overhead. A light clicked on, activated by a pull-cord in the Captain's hand.

"It's very low-tech here, behind the scenes," the guard explained.

They seemed to be in some sort of closet. There were

hangers to either side of them, covered with tuxedos, sport coats, leisure suits, tunics, underwear, and Bermuda shorts—all made out of snakeskin. Roger realized this wasn't simply any closet. They truly had reached Doctor Dread's inner sanctum!

"The public area is there," said the guard in a low voice as he gestured ahead, "beyond that drapery."

But Roger had seen something else as he looked to where the guard was pointing. There, just thrown on the floor, was a box of Nut Crunchies!

Roger hadn't seen that cereal box in years—his favorite breakfast food as a child. The company had discontinued the cereal when Roger was in his later teens, replacing it first with Fruit Flavored Crunchies—which was terrible—and then Marshmallow Crunchies—which was even worse. A year or two ago, they had tried it again by bringing out Oat Bran Crunchies, but, for Roger at least, the magic was gone.

Now, though, Nut Crunchies was here again—the cereal that had helped him survive childhood. He picked up the box. It looked brand new, as if it had just come off the supermarket shelf. And, even better, it rattled when he picked it up, as if it was full of Nut Crunchies!

"Captain Crusader?" the guard asked. "What's the matter? We can't stop now—not when we're this close!"

Roger shook his head. No, of course not. He couldn't be stopped by a simple box of cereal—but there had to be some explanation as to how a box of Nut Crunchies had found its way into the citadel of ultimate evil. Maybe, Roger thought, they still made Nut Crunchies somewhere in the Cineverse. He had always thought of this place as magical, but—until now—he hadn't realized how magical.

Maybe, he thought, he should open the box.

"Captain Crusader?" the Captain of the Guard pleaded.

Roger looked up. Yes, the fellow was right. There would be plenty of time later to recapture his childhood through a breakfast cereal. Now, though, they had a Cineverse to save.

Roger decided he'd take the box along, for luck perhaps—

or maybe because, now that he'd found Nut Crunchies again, he couldn't bear to let them go.

He walked forward to the heavy curtain that separated the closet they were in from the next room. It was time for Captain Crusader to take control.

"Yip?" Dwight said from nearby. Roger wondered if the dog wanted some Nut Crunchies.

Roger was about to step through the curtain, when the Captain of the Guard grabbed his arm. Roger glanced over and saw the guard shake his head. Roger stepped back.

"Do you hear somebody talking?" he whispered.

"Worse than that," the guard replied, also in a whisper. "I hear somebody—hesitating."

So they were one room away from Doctor Dread. Roger swallowed. It had all happened so fast. Was it time for the ultimate showdown?

Then the curtain moved aside. Another guard stood in the doorway, staring at them. And, beyond the guard, stood Doctor Dread himself.

"Roger—" Doctor Dread began, "or should I say—Captain Crusader? We've been waiting ever so long for your—" he paused suggestively—"arrival. I insist that you come on in and"—he hesitated darkly—"enjoy the party. It's a shame the party will be"—he paused with finality—"your last."

Roger stepped forward. The ultimate showdown was not beginning well.

21

Even though they were still surrounded by blue smoke, Louie knew they had arrived at their destination.

"Where you take us?" Zabana asked abruptly.

"How do you work this jewel?" Bouncer's one-track voice asked from the fog.

"And what about us other bunnies?" a high-pitched voice interjected.

"Yeah," another high-pitched voice added. "We haven't seen any action at all yet!"

"Bunnies thrive on action!" yet another high voice added.

"And don't forget hopping!" some other bunny piped up. "Bunnies also thrive on hopping!"

"Carrots, too!" somebody else chimed in. "Bunnies thrive on—"

"Yes, this is certainly educational," Louie interrupted brusquely, realizing that if he didn't, the bunnies might go on forever. "However, in a place like this, it's probably safer to be quiet."

That shut them all up. Now that the bunnies had halted their diatribe, it was remarkably quiet here, with only the distant sound of crickets. Of course, considering where they were, even crickets could be dangerous.

Still, they hadn't been attacked by the forces of Doctor Dread. Louie hoped that meant they had landed someplace relatively safe.

"I think we're safe here, for the moment," Louie said as the smoke dissipated around them. "I've brought us here to find Doctor Dread. While I was in his service, I learned about any number of the evil fiend's hideouts, but there are only three of those hiding places both large and well-protected enough to serve as Doctor Dread's true headquarters."

"Three?" Zabana asked helpfully. "What are three?"

"Does anybody know how to work this jewel?" Bouncer added hopefully.

Louie decided to answer Zabana's question.

"Their old headquarters is called the Citadel of Dread—a fortress full of peril for the unwary—but the place is too obvious. They'd expect us to go there first, so I didn't."

All but the last wisps of smoke vanished, and Louie saw that he and his fellows had materialized on a plateau above the jungle, with the great, red sun just rising over the horizon. The others were all watching him, nodding as if what he was saying made sense—which Louie hoped it did.

"Of course," he continued, "there's also Moon Base Zeta. That place is huge, and except for the occasional hideous alien menace, it's quite safe." Louie shook his head to completely dismiss that possibility. "No, I thought they would come here, the last place they would think I would look, and the most potentially dangerous of all three locations."

"Hah!" the jungle prince commented. "Zabana laugh at danger!"

"Bouncer laughs at many things too," the large rabbit added jovially. "That's why Bouncer and Zabana are friends." He stared down at the ruby he still held in his paws. "You think the jewel would work if Bouncer laughed at it?"

The crowd parted to let Officer O'Clanrahan step forward from the point where, until this moment, he had been standing away from the others, muttering into his hands.

"Faith and begorrah!" the officer wailed. "We're not facing a dangerous fortress, or hideous moon beasties. Can you tell us what we will be facing?"

"I'm glad you asked," Louie replied enthusiastically, since questions like that did a lot to help the plot along. "We've landed on a prehistoric planet, seemingly forgotten by time itself, where creatures a hundred times the size of their modern-day counterparts roam the wild to rend and kill anything in their path."

"Oh," Officer O'Clanrahan replied with very little enthusiasm. "If you'll excuse me, I'm going off into the corner and mutter some more." He proceeded to do exactly that.

Doc had somehow managed to get to his feet. Louie hoped that meant the Westerner would be coming around to his senses soon.

"Where exshactly ish thish hideout?"

"In a great, underground cavern beneath the jungle," Louie explained. "Unfortunately, to reach the cavern we have to enter the jungle first."

"Jungle is Zabana's home," the Prince of the Jungle interjected helpfully.

"Not this jungle," Louie assured Zabana grimly. "Not unless you're—prehistoric."

As if in reply, a thunderous scream came from the vegetation below.

"WONK!"

"What that?" Zabana asked incredulously.

Louie had heard that sound before, but wished he hadn't.

"If I'm not mistaken," he explained, "I think that's the battle cry of the Great Fanged Toad. Twenty feet long from head to tail, the toad thinks nothing of eating humans as light, between-meal snacks. But, we know it's down there now. If we can move swiftly and silently, there's a good chance at least most of us will survive."

As if in answer to the first horrid noise, another monstrous cry erupted from far overhead.

"CHIRP!"

"Whatsh that?" Doc ventured, doing his best to look up at the sky without falling.

Unfortunately, Louie knew the answer to that question as well. "I'm afraid that noise belongs to the Horrendous Three-horned Chickadee! The great bird flies high overhead, searching for helpless prey that it can swoop down on and gobble up with but one gulp of its tremendous beak. But we know it's up there now, and if we keep our heads down, and move quickly and quietly—''

"Bouncer goes first! Bouncer has the jewel!'' The large rabbit took the lead, and began to hop down the well-marked path to the jungle.

"I guess we'd better go too,'' Fluffytail said with a notable lack of enthusiasm.

Louie glanced down at the listless rabbit. Overall, the bunnies had been pretty quiet since they had left their cartoon homeland. In his usual sidekick role, he would have picked up on that sort of thing right away, but this hero business was proving far too time-consuming for such subtle things as rabbit mood swings.

"Is something the matter?'' he asked.

"No, we bunnies are always cheerful''—Fluffytail paused to shiver—"when we're not scared out of our rabbit minds.''

"WONK!'' screamed the giant toad down below.

"CHIRP!'' replied the Three-horned Chickadee high overhead.

Louie had to admit that the rabbits had a point.

"Hey!'' the large rabbit's booming voice called back to Louie. "Bouncer sees a big cave down here!''

Oh, no! Louie thought. Not a big cave. He knew all too well what came out of big caves on this particular movie world.

"Bouncer!'' he called ahead frantically. "Get away from—'' But, judging by the noises coming from the cave mouth, he knew he was already too late.

"GWRAAR!''

"What in cave?'' Zabana demanded.

"That'sh even worsh than the lasht couple noishesh!'' Doc agreed.

Indeed it was, a cry that chilled your very soul. And Louie would know that fearsome cry anywhere.

Bouncer bounded back toward them. But there was something following the rabbit, a blurry yellow shape that made

Bouncer look no bigger than his smaller bunny brothers and sisters!

"GWRAARARRRR!" screamed the immense yellow blur.

Louie could stand it no more. No matter how horrible the truth, he had to tell the others:

"It's the giant Sabre-toothed Hamster!" Louie summarized. "And its coming right for us!"

"Bouncer's sorry he saw da cave!" the large rabbit called as he scampered in fright.

"GWRAARARRRR!" the hamster-thing roared from much-too-close behind the fleeing bunny.

"Maybe Zabana speak to hamster!" the Prince of the Jungle suggested. "Save Bouncer!" He cupped his hands around his mouth and uttered a mighty cry: "Chee chee ribbit ribbit chee!"

The Sabre-toothed Hamster didn't seem to notice. "GWRAARARRRR!" he commented as he bounded ever closer to Bouncer.

Zabana was horrified. "Prehistoric hamsters not speak same language. Bouncer doomed!"

"Does *anybody* know how to use Bouncer's jewel?" the large rabbit called out with some desperation.

"Bouncer's in trouble!" one of the rabbits agreed.

"It's up to us, guys!" Highjumper told the others.

Even Fluffytail nodded at that. "We have to face our fear. This looks like a job for—bunnies!"

"Yay!" Highjumper agreed. "Bunnies to the rescue!"

The six remaining rabbits bounced rapidly down the hill toward the marauding hamster.

Highjumper led the way. "Sabre-toothed hamsters might be strong—" he called as he leapt close to the startled behemoth's face.

The other bunnies followed Highjumper's lead.

"They may be fierce—" another brown and white spotted rabbit called as it jumped across the great hamster's back. The monster twisted around, trying to grab for the bunny with its great clawed forepaw. But the bunny was gone, and another rabbit leapt in its place.

"They could be angry—" The next bunny jumped near the hamster's face again. The terror twisted back, but both wildly swinging forepaws met nothing but air.

"But he's not as fast—" Fluffytail called, bouncing twice on the creature's backside. The hamster roared its fury.

"He's not as cheerful—" a snow-white bunny opined as it bounded so close to the hamster that it almost hit the monstrous nose.

"He's not as fluffy—" a solid gray bunny added as he hopped beneath the hamster's stomach.

"As bunnies!" All seven rabbits cheered together.

The Sabre-toothed Hamster was totally confused. It sat back on its haunches and wailed.

"Time for da exploding carrot!" Bouncer exclaimed joyfully. Louie saw there was a shiny orange cylinder in the large bunny's hand. Bouncer handed the tube to the totally befuddled hamster. Then all the bunnies ran.

BOOM!

It exploded in the monster's face.

"YELP!" the giant hamster remarked.

"Yay!" the bunnies all cheered together, a sight almost too cute for words, as the hamster swiftly retreated to its cave down the hill. "Bunnies win again!"

Louie hoped they had enough exploding carrots to cope with whatever else they might find as they descended to the jungle floor.

"Well, come on, folks. We'd better get a move on."

"You're not going anywhere!" a woman's voice commanded as they were all surrounded by blue smoke.

Louie was instantly disoriented. Had somebody else used the Captain Crusader Decoder Ring to transport them to another world? No, he could still feel the ring on his finger, and he was reasonably certain that this was the only ring that he or his companions possessed. The thickness of the smoke around them could mean only one thing: some other person or persons had used another ring to transport their group into the middle of Louie and his companions!

Louie had all too good an idea of who these newcomers might be.

"Ah hahaha!" came from the blue smoke. "Ah hahaha." Triumphant laughter, from giggles to guffaws. Dread's henchpeople had found them once again, in no time at all, and with such precision that they had transported themselves into their very midst! And Louie's forces were scattered across this plateau. There was no way, in the middle of this thick blue smoke, that he could gather them all together to escape again.

But there was something even worse, a nagging doubt that Louie had missed something he had been looking at all along, something that would answer the question that may have doomed them all:

How did Doctor Dread's forces always know where they were going to be?

The smoke cleared. It was even worse than Louie had thought. While the smoke had obscured their actions, each of Dread's minions had felt his or her way across the plateau to take one of Louie's fellows captive! Menge the Merciless held a deadly looking ray gun to Doc's head, while Professor Peril had his snub-nosed .38 pointed straight at Zabana's chest. Bouncer was far less than a whip-length away from Mother Antoinette, and Bertha had all the other bunnies neatly within her shotgun sights. Unless something dramatic happened, this time there really was no escape.

"So," Mother Antoinette said with a slow, evil smile. "It is over at last."

It looked to Louie like it was over, too, but he couldn't help himself. The plot-centered sidekick within had to know the answer.

"I have to know. How did you find us so quickly?"

Mother Antoinette glanced perfunctorily at her companions. "Well, we might as well tell them. There's no way they're getting out of this one, and I've been aching to explain for ever so long."

Aching to explain? Louie shivered. Only the vilest of

criminals had to explain things before they killed. The villainous transformation of Roger's mother was complete.

"Yes, you poor, pitiful heroes, thinking you had a chance at success," Mother Antoinette gloated, "when we knew where you were at every instant, like struggling fish on a line, and we only had to wait until the time was right to tug on our hooks and reel you in!" She waved at the police officer in their midst, the one other member of Louie's band not held at gun- or whip-point. "And it's all thanks to you, Officer O'Clanrahan!"

Louie's mouth fell open as he realized how he had been double-crossed. "You mean, when you were muttering back there, your ranting had a purpose!"

"Afraid so, m'boy." Officer O'Clanrahan shrugged. "I was workin' for the other side."

"Not you!" Zabana exclaimed in horror. "Not faithful companion of Wonder Dog!"

"And how'd you like to be playin' second fiddle to a Wonder Dog every single day o' your life?" O'Clanrahan demanded. "It's 'Say, isn't that Dwight the Wonder Dog this' and 'Hey, isn't that Dwight the Wonder Dog that' and never a good morning or how you doin' today to Officer O'Clanrahan! I couldn't take it anymore. One more helpful bark, and I swore I'd start to scream!" He buried his face in his hands.

"But then—" The policeman took a deep breath and looked up defiantly at his former allies, "—then I was free of him at last! Bertha had talked to me, you see, back on my old home turf, and offered me certain opportunities I'd be a fool to refuse. It was a little difficult acting on them while the Wonder Dog was still around, but once he went into the drink, well, I was free to pursue my piece of the action." He balled his hands into fists, his eyes wild with the passion of his words. "I had to do it, don't you see? Now, maybe someday, they'll say—'Isn't that Officer O'Clanrahan?' "

"Yes, we'll say that now!" Mother Antoinette added with a chuckle. "Isn't that Officer O'Clanrahan, whose help allowed the forces of evil to crush these pitiful heroes, and assured that the Change, and the Cineverse, belong to Doctor Dread!''

Louie looked grimly at his companions. ''That's it, then?''

Mother Antoinette considered his query. ''No,'' she said after a moment. ''There is one more question.''

''Which is?'' Louie asked despite himself.

''Where would you like to be shot?'' Antoinette replied. ''In the head or in the heart?''

Dread's minions laughed as if that was the funniest thing in the Cineverse.

Louie had thought they had been in trouble before. He was wrong.

This was real trouble.

22

Roger glanced at his surroundings as he walked towards Doctor Dread. He figured he had nothing to lose. He might find a means of escape someplace in this room, and besides, if it took him an extra moment to reach Doctor Dread, that would be an extra moment he would stay alive.

This place looked like nothing so much as a throne room, the sort of place where absolute rulers had audiences with their subjects before they decided to cut off somebody's head. Roger rubbed the back of his neck and wished his imagination wasn't quite so vivid.

The centerpiece of the room was a large chair on a raised dais—it really did look like a throne. The walls opposite the chair were hung with huge, ornate tapestries—each one depicting a scene of vileness or destruction in great detail. In one, a man in a Santa Claus suit wielding a hatchet ran after a family. Flying saucers destroyed the Washington Monument in another. There seemed to be a common theme to all these wall-hangings. In every one, wrong triumphed over right. Perhaps, Roger thought, all these hangings were depictions of the Change.

"I see"—Dread's eyes turned to the Captain of the Guard— "we have already uncovered—treachery."

Roger glanced back at the Captain. The guard looked most uncomfortable. "But, Your Awfulness! You have to understand, I was all set to obliterate this scum, when he opened his mouth and—said something!"

"Said—something?" Dread repeated drily.

"Well yes." Sweat ran down the Captain of the Guard's face. "He is Captain Crusader, after all, and he has this—uh—way with words."

"Way—with—words," Doctor Dread repeated with a nod.

Roger realized that the Captain of the Guard was in even more trouble than he himself was at the moment. This guard had been a valuable ally. Roger didn't want to lose him, either through Doctor Dread's coercion, or the more permanent possibility of obliteration.

It looked like it was time, once again, for Captain Crusader to step forward and be heard.

Roger cleared his throat. "A man may have a throne room," he said slowly and clearly, "but he still puts on his pants one leg at a time."

The look of panic on the Captain of the Guard's face was replaced by a peaceful smile. "See? Is that nice or what?"

"Yeah!" another guard agreed.

"We see your point!" a third guard added.

"Captain Crusader is our kind of guy!" the guards cheered together.

"Well, it certainly was a beautiful sentiment—" Doctor Dread paused in total confusion. "What am I saying? This man is—dangerous! It is obvious that we cannot—allow Captain Crusader to speak. He must be—dealt with, now!"

Dwight chose that moment to poke his head through the curtains.

"Yip?"

"Watch out, men!" Doctor Dread yelled, pointing a snakeskin-gloved finger at the canine. But he hesitated with a frown, and put down his pointing hand. "Oh, never mind. For a moment, I thought that was Dwight the Wonder Dog."

"Yip?" Dwight repeated.

That was the diversion Roger had been looking for! He jumped quickly behind the nearest tapestry. There was a narrow space back here between tapestry and wall, maybe three feet across, so that he could walk back here without being detected. There seemed to be a some sort of dark recess farther up along the wall, too. Could it be another hidden passageway? Maybe Roger could escape to fight another day!

"Where's—Captain Crusader!" Doctor Dread roared. "Guards! If you do not find him, there will be—consequences!"

Roger took a slow step toward the recess. Something rattled at his hip.

"Wait a second!" Doctor Dread yelled from the other side of the tapestry. "I heard—Nut Crunchies!"

Roger looked down. Oh, no. Unthinkingly, he had held onto the box of his favorite breakfast cereal, and now that box might be his undoing. Nut Crunchies were incredibly noisy—it had been one of the joys of his childhood to hear them clatter into the bowl. But now, he couldn't move a muscle without rattling. Even dropping the box would be far too noisy. All he could do was stand here, frozen, until Dread and his henchmen found him!

Wait. Maybe there was another way. If he squatted very slowly and very steadily, perhaps he could ease the box down to the ground.

"He's somewhere—behind the tapestries!" Doctor Dread hesitated authoritatively. "Find him, men, if you value your—position!"

Roger wouldn't let Dread's orders panic him. As much as he hated losing this breakfast cereal, his life was too high a price to pay. He bent his knees, slowly sinking toward the floor. If he could simply set down the box of Nut Crunchies, it was only a few steps to the secret passageway.

Dwight poked his head past the next tapestry. The dog stared at him.

"Yip?"

The box fell from Roger's startled fingers and fell noisily to the floor.

"There he is!" Doctor Dread screamed triumphantly. "Guards—apprehend him!"

Burly hands reached around the tapestry and grabbed him from either side. Roger was dragged roughly from his hiding place. He was in too much of a state of shock to put up much resistance. The once-great Dwight the Wonder Dog was now so addled that he had accidentally given Roger away! Well, Dwight and the box of Nut Crunchies gave him away, if you wanted to be technical. Roger knew he would regret dropping that box, but, from the triumphant grin on the face of Doctor Dread, he feared those regrets wouldn't last very long.

"Captain Crusader. Dear—dear Captain Crusader, champion of justice and"—his pause this time was especially gleeful—"Nut Crunchies. You must really like them, to allow a cereal to—betray you so. Well, I can arrange for you to spend your time with Nut Crunchies—forever!" He snapped his fingers. "Guards! Position—the prisoner."

The two guards holding Roger dragged him over until his feet were resting on a big, red X on the floor.

"Our time together has been so—pitifully short," Doctor Dread purred. "But that's the way the new Master of the Cineverse wants it!" His hand reached to the wall and grasped a lever. Roger quickly read the neatly hand-lettered cardboard sign attached to the lever by a sturdy hank of string: INSIDIOUS TRAP DOOR #3.

Roger saw the Captain of the Guard, held at gunpoint by another of Doctor Dread's minions. There would be no help there. The Wonder Dog walked out from behind a tapestry and wagged his tail.

"Dwight!" Roger called. "You're my last hope? Don't you remember?"

"Yip?" Dwight replied.

"Hehheh. Hehhehheh." Doctor Dread laughed fiendishly as he pulled the lever. A trapdoor opened beneath Roger's feet, and he plummeted down, to land in—what? Visions of sharp spikes and poisonous flatworms danced through his head, for once driving out all those reminiscences of past wives and girl friends.

He hit something soft enough to cushion his fall as the trapdoor slammed shut above. That meant, at least, that the sharpened spikes were out. He didn't move for a moment, waiting for the killer flatworms to crawl up and overwhelm him.

But nothing seemed to be crawling anywhere. Whatever

Roger landed on was totally inert. He decided he should try to twist around and determine what exactly was in here with him. His leg had twisted when he fell. He tried to straighten it out.

The leg sank into the mass beneath him. He pushed, panic-stricken, with his hands, and his arms sank in as well. This stuff felt totally dry, if perhaps a little sticky, but it had the same effect as quicksand, and he could feel his whole body slowly settling down, until the small, dry granules circled his waist, then his chest, then his neck.

He had to calm himself. He had gotten out of tight spots before, by thinking like a movie and obeying the Laws of the Cineverse. Perhaps he could stop his descent by inventing another pithy saying, or singing a cheerful verse or two of song. It was worth a try.

He opened his mouth, and it was instantly filled with the small, sticky granules. They were sweet to the tongue. Startled, he bit down. The granules crunched.

He realized then what Doctor Dread meant when he said that Roger would spend the rest of his life with his favorite breakfast cereal. Roger had been dropped into a bottomless vat of Nut Crunchies!

Roger chewed. They were still every bit as good as he remembered them. Well, at least he wouldn't starve.

Now, if he could only find a way to breathe.

23

But trouble, Louie had to remember, could come in many different forms.

"CHIRP!"

The horrible birdcall was much louder than it had been before.

Mother Antoinette was looking up at the sky. "What is *that*?"

"Oh, dear," Menge the Merciless answered. "I'm afraid its the Horrendous Three-horned Chickadee!"

"That's a chickadee?" Mother Antoinette replied in disbelief. "What do you do with a giant chickadee?"

"Mostly hope that it never sees you," Professor Peril added in his usual to-the-point manner.

"CHIRP!"

"I'm afraid it's too late for that now," Bertha said grimly. "It may be too late for all of us."

Louie looked up at last. The creature was every bit as horrible as he remembered it—although now, he was seeing it much closer than he ever had before. The bird was the size of a small blimp, covered with long, knife-like yellow feathers. Its head was merely the size of your average bar and grill, each eye as large as Bouncer or Zabana, its beak as wide as Main Street.

"CHIRP!" it called a final time. And then it dive-bombed straight for them!

"Zabana not even attempt to talk to that thing!" the jungle prince remarked in a tone of horrified wonder.

"Sure is a sobering sight," Doc agreed, his speech once again slur-free. Louie realized the very sight of the monster bird must have shocked the Westerner back to his senses.

"What are we going to do?" Menge wailed. "That thing is deadly!"

Mother Antoinette only grinned. "That thing may be deadly," she replied, "but it has never faced the whip."

With a cry of defiance, she lashed out at the rapidly descending creature.

"CHIRP?"

Startled, the bird pulled out of its deadly descent.

"Now," Mother Antoinette commented confidently, "we will see who truly rules this lost world."

But the great bird's dramatic attack had attracted something else's attention.

"WONK!" came the cry from the edge of the plateau.

Menge, Peril, and Bertha spun around, all talking at once.

"Is that what I think—" "It can't be—" "But it must—"

"It's the Great Fanged Toad!" they screamed as one. All three of them pulled their weapons and began to fire.

"Hey, guys," Louie whispered hastily to his suddenly unguarded companions. "I think its time to get out of here!"

"Sounds like a good idea to this here fella," Doc drawled as he pointed to the far side of the plateau. "Let's hurry over yonder and use the ring."

Zabana's brow wrinkled in thought. "Dread sneaky! We bring hostage of our own!"

He ran over and grabbed Officer O'Clanrahan.

"What?" the police officer protested. "Get your bloomin' hands—"

Zabana tucked O'Clanrahan under one of his arms and hurried back to the others. Dread's cohorts were far too busy dealing with giant toads and chickadees to pay any attention.

"Zabana show what happen to man who cross Prince of Jungle!" He flexed his muscles threateningly.

"No!" Louie objected. "We need his information. We were followed here—it was a trap! My guess is that when and if we made it down to the hidden stronghold beneath the jungle floor, we would have found it empty.'' He stared at the treacherous police officer. ''So I have one question for you, Officer O'Clanrahan—Where is Doctor Dread?''

The man in uniform didn't even struggle in Zabana's overwhelming grip. ''Mother of mercy!'' he wailed. ''How would I know?''

''He's in one of two places,'' Louie demanded, ''the citadel or the moon base! Tell me or I'll slap you around!''

O'Clanrahan shook his head. ''Citadel? Moon base? I haven't the faintest idea what you're talking about.''

Louie paused in his interrogation. Maybe being slapped around by a five-foot-high sidekick wasn't enough of a threat. Maybe he had to up the stakes, and present this fellow with something worse than being tucked in Zabana's armpit.

''Perhaps,'' Louie suggested, ''you'd like to eat one of Bouncer's exploding carrots?''

''Yay!'' the large rabbit cheered. ''Bouncer likes da exploding carrots!''

''Why,'' Officer O'Clanrahan stuttered, ''f-f-faith and begorrah, how could I know where he'd be, but the—''

Bouncer pulled a metallic-looking carrot from somewhere under his fur.

''—the moon base,'' O'Clanrahan finished hastily. ''He's got to be at the moon base!''

The short sidekick stared up at the heavily perspiring Officer O'Clanrahan. Could he trust this double-crossing police officer? Louie guessed they'd have to wait and see. Still, every moment they couldn't find Doctor Dread was another moment closer to the height of the Change.

Louie had made his decision. ''All right, folks, let's get out of here. And don't let O'Clanrahan go!''

CRACK
CRACK *CRACK*
CRACK *CRACK* *CRACK*

Mother Antoinette's whip danced, trimming razor-sharp feathers here, drawing blood from the Three-horned Chickadee's beak there. Enraged, the giant bird tried to attack again and again, but everywhere it flew it found nothing but biting, naked leather!

"CHIRP!" the bird demanded, doing its best to stay aloft on its damaged wings. "CH-CHIRP!"

The monstrous Chickadee must have realized then that it was doomed. It spread its knife-sharp talons and fell from the sky in a final, suicidal dive, straight for the woman with the whip. It might die, but it looked like it would take Mother Antoinette along!

Mother Antoinette, however, had other ideas. She jumped to one side and tossed the whip into the air to meet the bird's rapidly descending claws. The leather wrapped itself around the bird's feet as she pulled on the whip handle, throwing all her weight behind it.

"CHIRP!" The great bird tumbled end over end, totally out of control. "CHIRRRRRRRRRRRR—" Its final cry was cut off abruptly as it crashed, beak first, into the caked mud of the plateau a scant foot from the spot where Mother Antoinette had been thrown to the ground by the force of her effort.

She picked herself up and brushed off the dirt, pausing for a moment to pat away the few petite drops of sweat that beaded her brow.

"My, that was fun."

The whip came free of the dead bird's feet with a single tug. She turned to see how her allies were doing.

Their monster, which looked like nothing so much as a really big toad with really sharp teeth, was down, too, rolling around in what Mother Antoinette assumed had to be its death agonies.

"WON—" it moaned. "WOO—WAAaaaa—" And then it moaned no more.

Menge, Peril, and Bertha turned to look at Mother Antoinette. They all appeared to be a little the worse for wear from their encounter. Their faces were dirty, their clothes torn. Peril had blood running from his nose.

"It took fourteen slugs," Peril summarized as he wiped

at his face with an Army green handkerchief, "twelve shotgun rounds, and eight blasts from the ray gun, but we've downed the thing at last."

"Good enough!" Mother Antoinette said approvingly. "We'll show these monsters they're no match for the combined forces of Doctor Dread! Woe be the man or monster who stands in our way!" She frowned and turned around quickly. "Speaking of men, what's happened to our captives?"

"Looks like they made good their escape while we were fighting these things," Peril surmised reasonably.

"The scum have escaped?" Mother Antoinette was upset enough to use a four-letter word. "Drat! Wait until we catch up with them. They'll not only wish they never got away, they'll wish they never had been born!" Her fury grew when she realized who else was missing. "Has O'Clanrahan vanished, too?"

Bertha nodded her head. "Never trust a traitor."

Mother Antoinette raised her whip over her head. "This has gone too far! No one crosses Mother Antoinette"—she stalled sinisterly—"without retribution! It all comes from our following Doctor Dread's foolish plans, when we should be pursuing"—she demurred daringly—"my destiny!" She lowered the whip to take it in both her hands. "Mother Antoinette is going to take"—she paused purposefully—"total charge!" She looked at each one of her allies—no, from now on, they were her underlings!

"Any objections?" she asked.

But her companions were too busy quivering and studying their shoes to raise any further points.

"Fine." Mother Antoinette answered the silence with a smile. "Then, let us go back to the Citadel of Dread and—rearrange a few things. There'll be no more hesitation, now! It's amazing, how different the citadel will become, with a mother's touch!"

She laughed as all four of them were surrounded by blue smoke.

24

Out of all the journeys Delores had taken through the Cineverse, this was, if not the most difficult, certainly the most peculiar.

"Bawwk!" Edward exclaimed from his position just ahead. "Sorry. I keep bumping my knees."

"Baahhhh," she reassured him. "Ther-r-re's no apology necessary. Please, let's keep moving."

This dark place seemed to go on forever, on a surface that always sloped slightly upward. And there was only a narrow pathway on which they could walk, perhaps the width of the two of them side by side. If they strayed from the path, they would stumble into sharp bits of what felt like metal and wood, the corners of something that Delores guessed might be furniture. But, with her transmogrified senses, she could be sure of nothing.

The floor beneath them was sticky in places as well, so that her feet—or whatever she now had that passed for feet—would make a sucking noise when she pulled them free. Between clucking noises, Edward said that this sticky part of their surroundings, at least, reminded him of home. Delores found no comfort in that thought. But at least there were no bubbling swamps here, or terrifying creatures roaring in the night. There was only this never-ending aisle, and the sticky floor beneath their feet. So she followed Edward upward, ever upward.

"Bawwwk!" Edward mused. "I had heard of this place. But I never thought I would see it—well, perhaps I'm not seeing it, considering the darkness and—Ouch! But I certainly feel it. My knees will never—bawwk—be the same. Who would ever think that I—a slime monster of humble beginnings—would end up in a place on the edge of the Cineverse?''

Once again Delores felt an odd sort of sympathy for the Slime Monster—or former Slime Monster. She knew the feeling was misplaced. This was the creature who transmogrified her and got her into this situation in the first place, after all. Still, she supposed she could talk to him about their present predicament.

''Maybe it had something to do with the Change.''

Edward made a noise that was half a chuckle, half a cluck. ''By now, everything has something to do with the Change. That's the very nature of the phenomenon: worlds collide and shift into other worlds, creating things that were never meant to be. And, of course, those new worlds create new changes. The very fact that we and the others have been bouncing from world to world may have brought about the Change that much faster.''

Delores was horrified by the thought. ''So, by trying to stop the Change, we've actually accelerated it?''

''Who's to say?'' Edward mused.

''So heroes will die, lovers part forever, and evil reign triumphant, all because of us?'' Delores could feel herself getting really upset.

''Not necessarily,'' the monster replied. ''I do not think the Change, in itself, is good or bad. It is only different. It is what those within the Cineverse do with the Change that tips the balance. Last time the Change ran rampant in our midst, Doctor Dread and his cohorts prevailed for a short time until at least some order was restored. And perhaps evil will win again. But it might be within our power to prevent it.''

Delores was astonished. She was discovering new philosophic depths in the muck-creature. ''You really are well-read, aren't you?''

''I have hidden depths,'' the Slime Monster agreed.

''But why didn't you tell us all this before?''

Edward sighed. ''When a slime monster is love smitten, all else is forgotten. And perhaps my hidden depths are gone, now that I've turned into a chicken.''

All things were possible, Delores thought. And she realized there might be a positive side to that statement as well as the negative.

She had another question: "Will we ever get out of here?"

"I think," Edward answered thoughtfully, "if we believe strongly enough, we will find the exit sign."

"Believe?"

"Yes, just as you believe that right must triumph over wrong, that lovers will be united in the end, that evil will, at last, be punished. All of the Cineverse is based on belief." Edward paused, clucking softly to himself. "Look for the exit sign, Delores."

Delores looked ahead, and saw a faint, red glow.

"There!" she called. "Do you see it?"

"I do now," Edward replied.

Without another word, they hurried up the aisle. As they got closer, Delores could indeed read the sign: EXIT

She could see Edward's silhouette in the crimson light. He seemed to be much the same size as before, but he had acquired something on his head that at first she mistook for a narrow, floppy hat but then realized was a cockscomb—the kind you saw on roosters. She didn't dare look down at her own hands and feet.

Edward had reached the door.

"Where will this take us?" she asked.

"Who knows?" he replied. "It may lead anywhere in the Cineverse. Perhaps it will open to anyplace that we want to go."

"I'd like to go find Roger." If anyone could put things right, she thought, it had to be Captain Crusader.

Edward did not reply for a moment. "Then again," he said, "we may open this door and find the real void, and be pulled from the Cineverse forever."

There was a choice to be made here, Delores realized, but it really wasn't any choice at all. She could not spend the rest of her life as a sheep.

It was time to open the door and find out.

25

Roger couldn't breathe. But Roger could chew and swallow. If he was going to die, it would be with a stomach full of Nut Crunchies.

He ate. And then he ate some more. Amazingly, he didn't feel deprived of oxygen. Actually, with every new sugar-coated Crunchie that entered his system, he felt better—younger, more full of energy, ready to take on the world, or the Cineverse! Perhaps it was merely the incredibly high sugar content of the Nut Crunchies that was imbuing him with such a feeling of power, but Roger suspected it was far more than that.

By choosing this method of disposing of Captain Crusader, Doctor Dread may have made a fatal mistake. Nut Cruchies were more than a breakfast cereal. They were a way of life!

Roger chewed and swallowed even more rapidly than before, feeling the Nut Crunchies expand in his stomach. What he wouldn't give for a nice cold glass of milk to go with all this cereal—but no, all thoughts of a balanced breakfast had to be left behind. He had a job to do.

For the first time, he truly felt like Captain Crusader.

The Nut Crunchies fell away as Roger detected a faint but discernible glow emanating from somewhere within this pit. It took Roger a moment to realize that the light was coming from him, his skin glowing with Nut Crunchie nutrition.

He lifted his head to regard the trapdoor overhead.

"Breakfast is the perfect way to start the day!" he shouted.

The trapdoor slammed open.

"Always brush your teeth and wash behind your ears!" he called.

Somehow, he flew from the pit and landed a dozen paces away from Doctor Dread.

"But—that's—impossible!" Dread hesitated in horror. "You should have—wallowed to death in Nut Crunchies by now!"

"You forgot, Doctor Dread," Roger replied with the slightest of smiles. "Nut Crunchies are Captain Crusader's friend."

"Curses!" Doctor Dread swore. "I will not be—defeated now. Not when—the Change—is so close!" He waved both his snakeskin-clad arms wildly. "Guards! He must be stopped—at all costs!"

All the guards in the room, including Roger's former ally, the Captain, rushed to grab him.

Roger raised a chiding finger. "Remember. Pushing and grabbing aren't polite."

The guard in the lead hesitated. "Hey! He's right!"

"*Don't* listen to him!" Dread insisted. "Grab him!"

The guards again rushed forward.

"Running and playing are great ways to let off steam," Roger reminded them, "after your homework's done."

This time, the first three guards stumbled to a halt.

"Gee, I hadn't thought of that," one of them murmured.

"There's this math problem I never *could* get," another agreed. "If you're traveling from station A at a constant speed of—"

"*Don't* let him talk!" Dread interrupted the problem-solving. "Gag him!"

The Captain of the Guard shook his head. "Yeah, you can't let him say any more of those—things. That's what got me the last time. Shut him up and we'll be safe to obliterate at our leisure."

"Even better!" Dread exclaimed with a sudden smile. "Cover your ears while you attack!"

The three guards in the lead all put fingers in their ears as they rushed forward. Roger stood his ground.

"A smile is the best way to say hello," he remarked as the guards approached.

"That makes a lot of sense," the Captain of the Guard muttered as he shook his head. But the other guards were almost on top of Roger now, all three humming (in addition to plugging their ears) so that they might be immune to Captain Crusader's awesome power.

"Three against one is never any fun," Roger said quickly.

"Yeah!" the Captain enthused. "What a good way to express it!"

"He does make a lot of—" Doctor Dread began. He punched a fist into his leg, as if forcing himself to wake from a dream. "No! Guards! Grab him now!"

But the guards were having problems as they realized they couldn't grab Roger with their index fingers already occupied.

The first guard unplugged his ears.

"To hear a good idea," Roger said quickly, "you have to listen."

The guard stopped and smiled. "Wow."

"How could I have ever doubted?" the Captain of the Guard shouted. "How could I have ever thought of going back to Doctor Dread?"

"Guards!" Dread called with rising panic. "*Don't* take your fingers from your ears. Push him back to the blue X!"

The two remaining guards obeyed, both bumping against Roger so that he stumbled back. He looked beyond his attackers, and saw Dread laugh quickly as he grabbed a lever, neatly labeled: INSIDIOUS TRAP #7.

Roger looked up, to see something hurtling down on him from above. He covered his head, but whatever it was crashed around him.

He opened his eyes, and realized he was surrounded by some sort of clear, glass cylinder. Did Doctor Dread think a puny prison like this could hold Captain Crusader?

But then Roger saw Doctor Dread laughing, and realized he could not *hear* Doctor Dread laughing. Maybe—if no one could hear his Captain Crusader sayings—maybe Roger was trapped after all! Still, there were other possibilities. Perhaps his Nut Crunchie-derived power would allow him to tip over this glass prison or something. He leaned against one curved wall, putting all his weight behind it. It didn't budge. Roger realized he'd better come up with that something pretty soon, or he would be in real trouble.

He looked back out of his prison, and saw there was a brand new commotion going on in Dread's throne room. Voluminous clouds of blue smoke were billowing from the far corner of the room. It must be Doctor Dread's henchpeople, returning to share in their leader's triumph. Would Roger's mother be with them? This was getting worse and worse.

Could this be the end of Captain Crusader?

26

Louie knew he'd made the right choice when he heard the diabolical laughter.

"Someone laughing on moon base?" Zabana asked.

"We didn't go to the moon base," Louie replied as the smoke cleared. "We went to the Citadel of Dread."

"Mother of mercy!" Officer O'Clanrahan. "I've been found out!"

"Never trust a turncoat," Doc offered sagely.

But Louie no longer had time to worry about the ethics of Officer O'Clanrahan. From the moment he heard that diabolical laughter, he knew they were in the presence of Doctor Dread.

The snakeskin-suited master of evil spun about to glare at the newcomers.

"Who dares?" His tone shifted suddenly as he got a look at Louie's companions. "B-b-bunnies!"

"Yay!" Fluffytail cheered. "It's Malevelo! Are we going to have fun today!"

"M-M-Malevelo?" the evil leader sputtered. "I am not—Malevelo! I am—Doctor Dread!" He took a ragged breath, pulling his gaze away from the rabbits. "Guards! Forget about Captain Crusader! Deal with the b-b-bunnies!"

Captain Crusader? Did that mean that Roger was here, too? Louie quickly looked around the room. Yes, there he was, trapped inside what looked like a giant, upside-down glass test tube.

"Bouncer!" he called. "Do you still have some of those exploding carrots?"

The large rabbit nodded his head eagerly. "Bouncer has lots of exploding carrots!"

Louie wondered for an instant where Bouncer stored all those deadly vegetables. Unfortunately, now was not the time to ask.

"Let your friends handle Malevelo for a minute," he instructed the large bunny instead. He pointed to Roger. "I need you to use your exploding carrots to free that fellow over there."

"Yay!" Bouncer replied. "Bouncer goes to free da fellow!"

In the meantime, Dread was pulling on a long, tasseled cord to which was tied a neatly lettered sign that read EMERGENCY GUARD ALERT! And the guards had been alerted. They were streaming in through doors at both ends of the room.

"Zabana! Doc! We need to hold off the others while the bunnies get to Doctor Dread!"

The Prince of the Jungle flexed his pectorals. "Zabana ready for anything!"

"Hoo-doggies!" Doc added with an enthusiastic whistle. "We finally ended up someplace where I can use my old six-shooters." Faster than Louie could follow, he drew both his pearl-handled revolvers. "Let's see how these fellas handle a couple a guns a'blazin'!"

The two of them stepped forward to confront the three dozen or so guards that had so far made it into the room. Louie figured the two sides were more or less evenly matched.

In the meantime, the six smaller bunnies had made their move toward Doctor Dread.

"Wait!" the ultimate master of evil shouted. "There's got to be a simpler way to work out our differences. Wouldn't you b-b-bunnies like some nice—carrots or something?"

"Why, thank you," Fluffytail replied, hopping closer to Doctor Dread.

"Maybe later," Highjumper added as he bounced on Fluffytail's heels.

"But for now," the next bunny continued as it, too, hopped along, "we want to play!"

"P-p-p-play?" Doctor Dread managed. "But—I don't—want—"

"We'll hop and skip and jump—" the fourth bunny sang merrily.

"And caper and cavort and frolic and frisk—" the next rabbit went on.

"And gambol and prance and rollick and romp—" the sixth rabbit proceeded.

Doctor Dread threw his arms in front of his face. "No! No! I won't listen! *Urk*!"

"You don't have to listen," Fluffytail replied.

"You just have to join in," Highjumper added.

"Bunnies are so much fun to play with," Bunny Number Three remarked.

"We're so soft and fluffy and pet-able," Bunny Number Four chimed in.

"And cute and adorable and charming—" Bunny Number Five said brightly.

"No!" Doctor Dread screamed. "No more! *Urk*! Have pity! *Ulp*!"

But the bunnies would show no mercy.

"And big eyes—" Number Six pointed out.

"B-b-big!" Doctor Dread wailed.

"And pink noses—" Fluffytail mentioned.

"P-p-p-pink!" Doctor Dread moaned.

"And big, cottony tails—" Highjumper insisted.

"C-c-ca—c-c-ca-cottony?" Doctor Dread stiffened, then slowly removed his arms from the front of his face. He no longer looked upset. In fact, he appeared to be almost comically angry.

"Rats!" he yelled, raising his fists in the air. "Malevelo will get those fluffy bunnies yet!"

"Cover your heads!" Bouncer's voice drew Louie away from Doctor Dread's amazing transformation. "Bouncer set da timer on da exploding carrot!"

Louie covered his head.

The carrot exploded.

Some time ago, Roger had stopped being truly surprised by anything that happened in the Cineverse—but what was happening now came close.

A very large rabbit had shown up and placed what looked like a metal carrot at the base of his prison. A moment later, all the glass had shattered and fallen away, and Roger was free at last. He stepped carefully over the surrounding pile of broken glass, into total chaos.

It wasn't simply the battle raging around him that Roger found confusing. No—the music was back, too. But it was all kinds of music at once—horns and violins and drums and blaring clarinets and even a couple of vocals, all struggling to be heard!

But there was more. The greatest cloud of blue smoke Roger had ever seen had erupted in the very center of the room. And out of that cloud came the voice of his mother.

"All bow before Mother Antoinette!"

"Hey!" Doctor Dread shook his head, as if waking from a dream. "What am I talking about?"

And then another voice shouted from inside the cloud:

"Make way for Hippolita, the Oracle of Venus!"

"Hey!" This time Roger recognized the tones of Menge the Merciless. "What are they doing in here?"

"Yes!" the ultimate master of evil yelled, a note of triumph returning to his voice. "I'm Doctor Dread! And no bunnies are going to make me feel any different!"

A warm male voice, rather like that of a travel guide, spoke next from the cloud:

"We happy villagers have finally found a way to leave our island paradise!"

"Hey! Where did *they* come from?" Bertha's voice demanded.

The next voice that emerged from the fog was one Roger had hoped never to hear again:

"Gnud fussin beverly, cuten slashen voola-voola!"

"What?" Professor Peril's voice economically demanded. "That person's not even speaking English!"

The smoke cleared, and Roger saw all the triumph leave Doctor Dread's countenance.

"Oh, no!" Dread screamed. "It's here! Before we were—truly ready! The height of—the Change!"

27

Of course, Louie had always suspected this sort of thing could happen. Whenever you used a Captain Crusader Decoder Ring, there was always a certain suspense in traveling from one world to another, a certain fear that the mix of different folks from different worlds would totally screw up the plot.

"Avast, me hearties!" a boisterous male voice called. "There's plenty of plunder here, for valiant buccaneers!"

But here it was, Louie thought, now, in the flesh, smack dab in front of him. Too many people from too many different places—all the characters working with Captain Crusader, and all of Dread's bad guys—and all had come to this citadel at the same time. And it was too much for the Cineverse to take.

"All right, men!" a grizzled sergeant yelled to his troops, "its time for us to take that hill!"

"Jumpin' Jehoshaphat!" Doc exclaimed as he ran after the soldiers. "I knew I was needed here for something!"

And all those people from all those places had led to something else, like a hole in the Cineverse. More people were showing up, from a hundred different movie worlds, almost as if they were somehow being dragged here. And, Louie guessed, they were—by the Change.

"Hey, Roger Dodger!" a blond teenager in loud bathing trunks announced. "Surf's up!"

Louie hadn't been near the middle of the Change before. In fact, the last time around, he hardly noticed the Change had happened until some of the good guys started getting plugged.

Something trumpeted.

"Is fear-maddened elephant, from Zabana's home jungle!" the Prince of the Jungle announced. "Is no place like home!" The mighty muscleman took off after the rampaging pachyderm.

This time, though, the Change looked like it was going to be a lot worse than before. This time, *everything* was changing. Even after the blue smoke had cleared, people—and animals—were showing up from everywhere—and it was already changing Doc and Zabana and the others who were already here.

This, Louie suspected, was what Doctor Dread had wanted to happen all along. But could even the greatest evil mastermind in all the known Cineverse handle this kind of a mess?

There was too much happening here. Louie had to keep his wits about him, until somebody got control of this, or they were all in trouble.

And then somebody started to sing.

> "Oh, its such a sunny day,
> Those nasty clouds beware!
> Come on, fellas, walk with us,
> We're going to the fair!"

Louie realized his mouth was watering. Maybe, if he went with these brightly dressed folks, he'd get a chance to judge the pie-tasting competition!

No, no, there were other things he had to do first. His wits—he was keeping his wits. He'd remember what he had to do if he looked around the room. Oh, yeah, he always wanted to learn how to use a sword. Or maybe it was time to finally get on that board and surf!

What had he forgotten? Oh well, he'd figure it out in a moment. He curled his hand around an imaginary sword. Whatever else happened, he had to make sure, at all costs, that he wasn't affected by the Change.

• • •

Roger had to concentrate. It was almost impossible with all the noise and music, not to mention what was happening to his companions. Zabana had run off to chase an elephant, Doc seemed to have joined the Army, and Big Louie appeared to be trying to surf while he was holding a sword.

"Yip?" Dwight asked behind him. The Wonder Dog appeared to be so far gone that he didn't even notice the chaos around him.

But, if Dwight could separate himself from the mess here, so could Roger. He just had to take a deep breath and think like Captain Crusader. Why, only a few minutes ago, he was spouting prime Captain Crusader sayings for every occasion. There was no reason, save for all this distraction, that he couldn't do it again.

And Roger would do it! Even in his addled state, it looked as if Dwight the Wonder Dog had once again saved the day!

"Good boy!" Roger called.

"Yip?" the Wonder Dog replied.

Now, if Roger could simply come up with a Captain Crusader saying all-encompassing enough to deal with what was going on around him—

"Back!" a woman shouted. "Back, I say!" Roger turned his head to see a gang of pirates being held at bay by a black-clad woman with a whip.

That black-clad woman was also Roger's mother.

All thoughts of Captain Crusader left Roger's mind as he watched the whip in action. She was quite good at it, flipping it back and forth to keep a trio of musclemen at bay. It was a side of his parent that he had never seen before. Perhaps, he thought, he'd been guilty of taking his mother a little bit for granted.

But a new group was taking an interest in the woman in black. "Avast, me hearties!" the leader of the pirates leered at Roger's mother. "Here's a prize worth taking."

Actually, when Roger took a closer look at the group of twenty or so menacing his mom, he realized they weren't all strictly pirates. Somehow, a half-dozen surfers seemed to have gotten mixed in, too. But they were all acting like pirates, and there must have been close to two dozen of them. Roger considered going to his mother's aid. She *was* his mother, after all, even though she was working for the other side, and she might be able to manage three assailants—but twenty?

CRACK

One look at the way his mother was handling her newest attackers, however, and he gave up any thoughts of rescue.

CRACK *CRACK*

Besides, he didn't want to get too close to that nasty weapon of hers.

CRACK *CRACK* *CRACK*

His mother snapped the whip, curling it around the pirate captain's leg and pulling him from his feet.

"I am nobody's prize!" she declared. "I am Mother Antoinette!"

"Ah, what spirit!" The pirate captain laughed. "She is a beach bunny worth pursuing!"

Beach bunny? Roger frowned. Something was wrong here. He'd seen enough pirate movies to know. Shouldn't the proper pirate term for a desirable woman be "wench" or "vixen"?

CRACK went his mother's whip. *CRACK* *CRACK*

One pirate cried in surprise as his hoop earring was pulled from his ear, while another brigand pointed in surprise to the place where the whip had sheared his wooden leg in half.

Roger's mother laughed, and the whip swept in wide circles above the pirates' heads.

CRACK *CRACK* *CRACK*

In a matter of seconds, half a dozen pirates had lost their scraggly beards.

"Enough is enough!" the pirates yelled.

"We yield!"

"Shiver me timbers, it is a bummer!"

Bummer? There it was again, that intermingling of surfer and pirate. Now that he thought of it, Roger remembered there had been a similar mixing of worlds during the first Change, when genres combined into things like space Westerns and spy musicals. The results were never very good, and could be explosively bad! And here it was, happening all over again.

Roger was beginning to wonder if it might already be too late for the Cineverse to be saved.

"Beggin' your pardon, Captain," one of the pirates said, "but maybe she'd consent to lead us?"

"Lead you?" Roger's mother chuckled darkly. "Very soon, Mother Antoinette will be mistress of everybody!"

"What?" Somehow, in all this noise, Doctor Dread had overheard the conversation. "You dare to—challenge my authority? I will show you—what happens—"

But Mother Antoinette's whip went to work before Dread could even stop hesitating. *CRACK* *CRACK* the whip replied, and Dread's snakeskin pants had been transformed into snakeskin Bermuda shorts.

"Well—" Dread hesitated, looking down at his pale and newly exposed knees. "Perhaps we can discuss—"

"But you have to talk to bunnies first!" Highjumper interrupted.

"*Urk*! *Ulp*!" Doctor Dread replied, his face contorting. "Malevelo doesn't talk to bunnies! Malevelo has bunnies for dinner!"

"Bunnies for dinner? Bouncer likes carrots!"

All seven bunnies, Bouncer included, hopped around the villain and laughed.

But, instead of the usual angry response, Doctor Dread only smiled. "Carrots? *Urk*! Malevelo—likes carrots. Malevelo especially likes exploding carrots!"

"Exploding carrot?" the very large bunny replied cheerfully. "Bouncer likes da exploding carrot, too!"

Dread's face once again convulsed, as if there were a great war going on within his skull. "*Urk*! *Ulp*! Malevelo—wants the exploding carrot!"

"Okay!" Bouncer replied with a big smile. "Malevelo is the boss!"

The big rabbit bounced over to the ultimate master of evil and handed him a carrot with a lit fuse.

"Oh, really," Doctor Dread said as he took the offering. "On second thought, I—couldn't."

He stuffed the carrot in Bouncer's mouth. Bouncer swallowed in surprise.

"Hehhehheh!" Doctor Dread chuckled triumphantly. " Malevelo—I mean, Doctor Dread—will show you what you can do with your exploding carrots! Now, if you'll—excuse me?"

Dread started to run.

"BURP!" Bouncer replied. "Oh, dear. You have to excuse Bouncer, too."

"What?" Doctor Dread demanded as he stopped his retreat. "I stuff one of your exploding carrots into your stomach, and all it does is give you—gas?"

Then Bouncer exploded. Where the rabbit had stood a moment before, there was now nothing but a great cloud of dark smoke.

Doctor Dread's laughter rose above everything else. "Yes! Take that—bunnies! You may force me into playing this stupid wizard, but—Bouncer is no more!"

"Oh, yeah?" a voice said as someone stepped from the cloud—someone wearing a trenchcoat, with a glowing cigarette hanging from his lower lip. "We'll see about that, Buster." As the figure emerged from the smoke, Roger realized that his lower lip, along with the rest of his face, including those long ears poking through the slouch hat, belonged to Bouncer!

"I'm glad you called me in," the raincoat-clad rabbit drawled. "It's my job as a gumshoe to find out—Who used the exploding carrot?"

It was Bouncer, and it wasn't Bouncer. Roger was fascinated. This must be the Change at work.

"Excuse me, doll-face," Bouncer remarked as he stepped past Roger's whip-wielding mother. "That's why I've called you all here today, to solve the mystery of—who killed Bouncer Bunny."

"No!" Doctor Dread screamed. "I won't have it! I—dealt with you, and now you won't—stay dead! I'll show you what happens to b-b-bunnies who—double-cross Doctor Dread!"

He ran to another one of his levers. This one read DEADLY WEIGHT RELEASE. Doctor Dread pulled the lever.

A ten-foot-square solid steel cube fell on top of the gumshoe bunny.

"Hehheh hehhehheh!" the mastermind laughed in nervous relief. " Mess—with Doctor Dread—would you? And I'll deal with all—you other b-b-bunnies, too!"

Dread's gloating was interrupted by a group of men and women, strolling arm in arm as they sang:

"Join us in our morning walk;
We're all without a care.
Sing a song, or hear us talk,
We're going to the fair!"

It seemed to Roger there were a lot more people strolling and singing than there had been a moment before. Yes, there was Zabana, with his hand on the trunk of his elephant! And, taking up the rear was the woman with the knife from the foreign art film! Amazingly enough, she was singing, too:

"Voola-voola beverly
Smashen kutz shaboom!
Minsky mensky stephanie,
Slashen gutz kadoom!"

Roger couldn't believe what he was seeing. Had the mad woman from the art film found peace at last? It would be a relief not to have to worry about her anymore. Through force of habit, as much as anything, Roger's eyes looked down to read the subtitle:

"Oh, its such a cheerful day.
My worries to avenge.
I'll laugh, I'll skip, I'll stab his heart,
And get my just revenge!"

Then again, perhaps Roger would rather keep his distance.

But something was happening to the steel cube. It had begun to rumble, and a crack was rapidly splitting the metal apart from top to bottom. The two halves crashed asunder, and once the dust settled, there stood Bouncer—but a different Bouncer. He was wearing army fatigues, with two ammunition belts crisscrossing his chest. He looked to Roger like nothing so much as the hero of one of those "One-man-against-an-entire-terrorist-army" movies.

"Yo," Bouncer said to Doctor Dread. "You're in trouble, now."

But Roger was letting himself be carried along by the course of events. If he was going to have any effect on his surroundings, he had to get his Captain Crusader act in gear.

"No b-b-bunny's going to get the better of me!" Doctor Dread shrieked.

Professor Peril stopped doing battle with some mounted cavalry to run to Dread's side. "Boss, get yourself together! You should know it's almost impossible to kill these cartoon bunnies. Even if you do, they'll just end up with wings and a harp, and they'll keep on bothering you!"

Roger was surprised at how much sense Peril made. The man knew his cartoons. But Doctor Dread was beyond reasoning as he ran to another of his myriad levers.

"Even mercenary-soldier bunnies cannot stand up to my deadly piranha pool!"

He pulled the DEADLY PIRANHA POOL lever. A trapdoor opened at Bouncer's feet. But the mercenary-bunny that Bouncer had become was too fast for Dread's machinations. He jumped back as the door sprang away. Roger could hear the deadly, bunny-eating fish churning about in the water, just out of sight. Bouncer pointed his AK-47 down into the pit and fired a dozen, quick bursts.

The piranhas thrashed no more.

"Yo," Bouncer said as he pointed to Dread. "You're next."

"No!" Dread's head whipped back and forth, searching for the lever that would conquer the unconquerable bunny. His right hand reached for GIANT DESCENDING PENDULUM while his left hand sought BOILING OIL RESERVES and he looked up at his SHORT-RANGE MISSILE CONTROL PANEL.

"No!" Dread screamed. "Any, or all, of them might fail. I need my greatest weapon. Mother Antoinette!"

Roger's mother paused from whipping some Roman soldiers. "Yes?"

"I need your help," Doctor Dread pleaded.

Roger's mother smiled at that—the same, small, cruel smile she used to use when she told Roger he had to finish his lima beans. "My help does not come—cheaply," she replied.

"I understand!" Dread screeched. "Anything you want! Just—deal with the bunny!"

"Anything—I—want?" Roger's mother turned to face the rabbit.

"Yo," Bouncer said uncertainly. "I don't want to hurt a lady."

Mother Antoinette flexed her whip. "You'll soon learn that I'm no ordinary lady."

CRACK

Bouncer jumped away from the dancing leather.

CRACK *CRACK*

But Mother Antoinette had forced him up against a wall. There was no place for the rabbit to go.

"Yo—" Bouncer began. But then the whip was everywhere!

CRACK *CRACK* *CRACK*

It slashed at Bouncer and the surrounding wall, as tapestry, masonry, and bunny fur flew and intermingled. Bouncer cried out incoherently as he was covered by cloth and brick.

There was a moment of total silence in the throne room.

Roger's mouth fell open. Bouncer was gone? If Captain Crusader could have said something, he might have been able to save the giant rabbit. If Roger could somehow get over his shock even now, he might be able to stop this madness from going any further.

"Heh heh," Doctor Dread laughed uncertainly at first, then with more vigor. "Hehheh hehhehheh! Mother Antoinette! Whatever your services cost, they are well—"

The debris that covered Bouncer shifted.

"What?" Roger's mother demanded. "It can't be. Not after—"

A bunny paw emerged from the mass of cloth and brick.

"Can't *anything* kill it?" Peril whispered.

A second paw broke free—and this paw was carrying a chainsaw.

It didn't surprise Roger in the least when, as Bouncer's face finally emerged, he was wearing a hockey mask.

It was Dread's turn to scream incoherently as he ran for the far end of the throne room.

But Roger realized what was happening now. He was watching the Change in action, as Bouncer was transformed from a rebel hero to an antihero to something that went beyond heroics. Roger knew that he had to stop this now, before it went any further.

He cleared his throat.

"A party is always more fun," he shouted to the surrounding throng, "when everybody obeys the rules!"

And everybody stopped.

What did Roger do now?

28

Mother Antoinette had to admit it. Her son made a lot of sense.

Somebody tugged at her sleeve. She turned to see the cringing form of Menge the Merciless.

"Don't you see what's happening?" Menge pleaded. "It's Captain Crusader. Don't listen to him!"

Mother Antoinette blinked. "Why not?"

"If you *listen* to him," Menge emphasized, "you'll start *believing* him."

"Well," she answered reasonably, "he is in public relations. He has a way with words."

Menge stopped cringing long enough to look her straight in the eye. "You'll have to give up your whip," he said simply.

Mother Antoinette felt like she had been splashed by ice-cold water. What was she doing listening to her son, anyway?

"Never!" she exclaimed with renewed conviction. "What do I have to do?"

Menge got that sort of sly smile that made him so attractive. "This is our time for triumph!" He flinched when he realized what he had said. "I'm sorry—*your* turn for triumph. I'm just happy to—um—follow you."

Sometimes, however, her Mengy could be quite exasperating. "*How* will we triumph?" she demanded.

"Oh, of course, Mother Antoinette!" Menge groveled. "It's time for the Buchanan Device!"

She had to admit, this sounded interesting. "The Buchanan Device?"

"Yes!" Menge agreed all over again. "We'll take the

Buchanan Device and—'' He gasped when he realized he'd made the same mistake again. ''Oh, mercy, Mother Antoinette. You, of course, will use the Buchanan Device—and I, perhaps, might be worthy enough to lick your shoes—''

Mother Antoinette nodded. ''Perhaps that can be arranged. But about the Device?''

''It's how Dread controlled the Change in the first place,'' Menge confessed in a low tone. ''Turn it on, and you can alter anything that you desire.''

That sounded even better to Mother Antoinette. ''It's that powerful?'' she asked.

''There's nothing more powerful in the Cineverse,'' Menge assured her.

Then, at last, Mother Antoinette could have everything exactly the way she wanted it. There was no time to delay. She glanced back at Menge. ''But how do we obtain this device?''

His sly smile was back. ''Depend on me. I know the device's secret hiding place.'' He waved for her to follow her across the room. They had to dodge a small boat of people wearing life preservers, and a conga line of dancing alligators, but Menge brought her at last to a tapestry of Wall Street bigwigs bilking their clients.

''It's back here,'' he confided. He pulled the tapestry out of the way. And, indeed, there, taped on the recessed wall, was a neatly hand-lettered, cardboard sign:

BUCHANAN DEVICE
SECRET HIDING PLACE
PRESS HERE

Mother Antoinette pressed the spot indicated. A wall the size of a garage door rolled out of the way.

''Step out of the way,'' Menge cautioned hastily, ''—uh—please?''

Mother Antoinette stepped back as a yellow machine the size and shape of a minivan—except that it had no windows and was equipped with about four dozen blinking lights—rolled forward.

It stopped directly in front of Mother Antoinette. She saw a small keypad on the side of the bulky machine. Directly above the keypad was a speaker, and another button, with a cardboard sign that read PRESS HERE.

Mother Antoinette pressed again.

The machine hummed to life.

"Welcome to the Buchanan Device," a cheery male voice announced from the speaker, "your one-stop shop for major plot alterations. If you want the good guys to win, press ONE. If you want the bad guys to become good guys, press TWO."

Neither one of those sounded like something Mother Antoinette wanted to do. She hoped there were better options farther down on the list.

A door opened on the side of the yellow device.

"A door?" Menge yelled in disbelief. "The Buchanan Device doesn't have any doors!"

"If you want all the good guys to fall in love, press THREE," the device's voice continued.

Two of the strangest creatures Mother Antoinette had ever seen stepped out of the doorway. Even though they both walked on two legs like humans, they looked far more like animals. The second creature actually looked like nothing so much as a sheep, although there might have been a smidgen of dog, cow, and perhaps half a dozen other mammals thrown in. The first creature, however, was so disgusting that it was difficult for Mother Antoinette to even look at it. Still, somehow, she forced herself. The future ruler of the Cineverse had to be tough. Ugh. The first creature looked exactly like a giant chicken covered with slime.

"If you want all the bad guys to fall in love, press FOUR," the machine went on. "If you want the bad guys to fall in love with the good guys, press FIVE."

"We're here at last," the Slime Chicken said solemnly. "Excuse me, but is this the Change?"

"If you want your entire plot overthrown by violent revolution, press SIX."

"Yes, this is the Change," Mother Antoinette agreed curtly, angered that the device wasn't giving her better choices. "Couldn't this machine work a little faster?"

Menge nodded. "They always leave all the best stuff for the end."

"If you want your world to end in a natural disaster, press SEVEN. If you want your world to end in an unnatural disaster, press EIGHT."

Mother Antoinette frowned. She really hadn't heard any option here that was particularly to her liking.

"If you want to wipe everything out and start all over again, press NINE."

Oh, all right, maybe if she listened to them again. She pressed NINE.

"No," Menge shrieked. "Not that!"

"Not what?" Mother Antoinette demanded. "I pressed NINE to start the machine over."

"But NINE doesn't start the machine over. It starts *everything* over!" Menge stopped to gulp air. "The Buchanan Device," he began again, only slightly less hysterically, "has an unlimited number of plot options. The villains start winning around fifteen or sixteen."

Oh, Mother Antoinette thought. Oh, dear. She always had trouble with the directions on these new electronic machines.

She looked over at Menge. "And there's no way to stop it?"

"There's no fighting the Buchanan Device! We are doomed! We are—"

Another man's voice interrupted Menge's panic. It was a voice she'd recognize anywhere—the voice of her son. "Mother, what are you doing?"

How could she answer him? Somehow, the whip in her hand didn't seem to mean that much when she had just destroyed the universe. Fortunately, Menge did the answering for her.

"Ah hahaha!" was Menge's reply. "It is too late! No mere Captain Crusader saying can stop the Buchanan Device!"

"The Buchanan Device?" Roger asked with that annoying little whine he sometimes got in his voice. "*Mother—*"

"Everything will be wiped out!" Menge continued. "The Cineverse will have to start from scratch. Maybe even we will die, but we will die triumphant!"

She did all that by pressing NINE? Oh, well. At least, Mother Antoinette thought, she got to keep her whip until the end.

29

The large yellow machine, the so-called Buchanan Device that his mother had activated, hummed dangerously.

"Haven't we been through this before?" a sheep that stood on two legs said with a woman's voice. For some reason, Roger found the sheep strangely attractive. Did this say something he didn't want to know about his sexual preferences? Fortunately, the situation was too desperate now for him to dwell on such matters.

The machine's hum grew even louder.

"I'm afraid so," answered the woman's companion, who was not attractive in the least. "Brawwk! You can't overuse a good plot device."

Roger recognized that dour voice. It was Edward the Slime Monster. But that meant that the sheep with Edward had to be—

"Delores?" he asked, looking into the sheep's big brown eyes.

But the sheep turned her head away. "Oh, Roger! I didn't want you to see me like this!"

"Nonsense, Delores!" Roger rushed forward to grab her hand, or forepaw, or whatever it was. "We're back together again. That's all that matters!"

"Baahhh—but I'm a sheep!" she protested.

Roger's hands sank deep into her woolly shoulders. "It's something we will have to rise above."

"Oh, dear," the thing that used to be Edward moaned. "I should have realized. Brawwk! They are reconciled, and the Slime Monster goes on—alone."

The Buchanan Device sputtered.

"Something's wrong!" Menge exclaimed.

The Buchanan Device groaned.

"Danger, danger," the pleasant male voice said from the speaker. "There is too much happening. We are in danger of cosmic overload. Remove six plot threads immediately or the Buchanan Device will explode."

Roger's mother stared at the machine. "Does that mean we won't go back to the beginning of the Cineverse?"

"Yes," the pleasant voice replied. "Instead, the Buchanan Device will overload, destroying itself and the entire world around it, in a tremendous fiery explosion."

"Oh," she replied. "Doesn't seem like much of a difference, does it?"

"Sorry," the Buchanan's speaker replied. "That's the way the plot goes sometime." It resumed humming, louder and higher than before, the kind of humming that always ended in explosions.

"Roger!" his mother yelled. "Do something!"

Yes, Roger thought, the only one who could save them now was Captain Crusader. "A machine is only as good as the person who uses it!" Roger yelled.

The humming became even more pronounced.

Roger tried again. "Uh—a clean machine is a happy machine! Um—electricity is a computer's friend!"

It was no use. Menge had been right—Captain Crusader sayings had no effect. The hum was becoming more hysterical with every passing second. What else could Roger do?

"Help!" he wailed.

There was a second of startled silence, as if the Cineverse had heard his call.

Roger realized then that the humming had stopped, and had been replaced by an angelic choir, as a bright blue chariot descended from the sky.

OKAY, THIS HAS GONE FAR ENOUGH!
IT'S TIME TO SETTLE DOWN!

Before he even saw the backlighting or the blue-smoke cigar, Roger realized it was the Plotmaster. He also realized that almost everybody around him had frozen, as if time stood still.

The blue chariot, which, as far as Roger could tell, was self-propelled, landed next to the now-quiet Buchanan Device.

HEY, ROGER BOOBALA,
BEFORE YOU CAN START THINGS UP AGAIN,
YOU GOTTA STOP 'EM FOR A MINUTE!

Roger was astonished. "You mean, you can just show up and—stop everything?"

HEY, ROGER BABY, LET'S FACE IT,
THE CHANGE CAN ONLY GO SO FAR.

"And you're just going to appear and fix everything?" Roger asked incredulously. "This is pretty *deus ex machina*, isn't it?"

HEY, I'LL BE THE FIRST TO ADMIT
SOME PLOTS ARE BETTER THAN OTHERS.

"So you're the Plotmaster?" Delores asked in wonder.

AND YOU MUST BE DELORES?

Wait! Roger thought. Why wasn't Delores frozen like the others?

The big backlit guy chuckled.

SOME PEOPLE HAVE CHANGED TOO MUCH FOR EVEN
THE PLOTMASTER TO HAVE ANY CONTROL OVER THEM!

"The Plotmaster." Even Edward the Slime Chicken was impressed.

"And you're going to fix everything?" Delores asked.

WELL, WHATEVER I CAN.
EVEN THE PLOTMASTER HAS LIMITS.

"No!" another woman's voice yelled. "I've come too far to be stopped now!" Roger's mother stepped forward.

CRACK went her whip.

UH-OH.
HERE'S ONE OF MY LIMITS NOW!

CRACK *CRACK*

The Plotmaster ducked as the whip waved over his head. When he spoke again, Roger thought he could hear real panic in his voice:

SHE'S LIKE YOU, ROGER.
SHE'S NOT FROM THE CINEVERSE.
I HAVE NO POWER OVER HER!

CRACK * CRACK* * CRACK*

The whip was everywhere. The backlighting flickered and died as the Plotmaster ducked inside his blue chariot.

His mother laughed. "Who's the ruler of the Cineverse *now*?"

The Plotmaster's voice echoed up from inside the Chariot.

ROGER?
I COULD USE SOME HELP HERE.

The Plotmaster needed him? But how could he do anything against Mother Antoinette? Even though she was one of the ultimate masters of evil, there was no way Roger could strike his mother!

But, he realized, there was another way. He tried to think of the best way to reach her.

"A clean room is a happy room," he said.

"What?" His mother stopped her whip, mid-crack.

Roger thought he heard someone else mutter from somewhere in the frozen throng. Could his Captain Crusader sayings be waking the others, as well?

His mother shook her head. "What's wrong with me? I have to finish somebody off—with the whip!"

Uh-oh. Roger had to say something else, fast.

"Your mother is only a phone call away."

The whip almost slipped from his mother's hands. She smiled. "Yes. I've often said that."

A six-foot-high bunny bounded out of the crowd and took off his hockey mask.

"Bouncer has been through some changes, too!" he declared.

That meant Roger *was* waking up the others! The more he exerted the power of Captain Crusader, the more normal the Cineverse became!

Mother Antoinette looked down at her hands. "A whip? I have a whip!"

Whoops. His mother's will was too strong to be controlled by any of his Captain Crusader sayings for long. The next one would have to be good.

"Plots may come and plots may go, but a boy's best friend is his mother."

"How nice of you to say so." The whip fell from Mother Antoinette's fingers.

The Plotmaster peeked over the edge of the chariot. Without the backlighting, he looked a little like the Masked Marshal.

ROGER, BABY,
AS WELL AS THIS WORKS—
IT'S ONLY A HOLDING ACTION.
YOUR MOTHER'S STILL BEEN ZAPPED BY THE ZETA RAY!

Edward the Slime Chicken shivered. "Brawwk? The Zeta Ray? Anything but—the Zeta Ray."

Roger stared at the Plotmaster. Maybe, he considered, the fellow actually looked a bit more like the Secret Samoan.

"The Zeta Ray?" Roger had almost forgotten about the foul machine that had turned his mother to a life of evil. Doctor Dread probably kept it around here somewhere. "Do you have any idea where it is?"

HEY!
I'M THE PLOTMASTER!
THE LEVER'S RIGHT OVER THERE,
NEXT TO THE ONE FOR THE TIGER PIT?

Roger looked where the Plotmaster pointed his cigar (which was still producing blue smoke). Oh, yes. Roger saw it now, right by that colorful tapestry showing the many uses of the cat-o'-nine-tails.

He looked back at the Plotmaster. "But won't exposing her to the Zeta Ray again simply make her more evil?"

The Plotmaster nodded.

THAT'S WHY YOU NEED THE JEWEL.

"The jewel?" Roger asked.

ASK BOUNCER.

The bunny brightened considerably as he popped the ruby from his navel. "Do you know how to use Bouncer's jewel?"

The Plotmaster nodded again.

DID YOU LOOK ON THE OTHER SIDE OF THE TAG?

The large bunny jumped up and down in anticipation. "Bouncer never thought to look on the other side!"

Roger looked over Bouncer's shoulder as the bunny flipped the ruby's tag over. There, under the washing instructions (GENTLE CYCLE, TOWEL DRY) were the following words: PLACE JEWEL IN ZETA RAY.

"Didn't I have a whip around here someplace?" Roger's mother declared suddenly.

IT'S NOW OR NEVER

the Plotmaster warned.

"Do it!" Roger yelled.

"Bouncer to da rescue!" the large bunny replied as he crossed the room in three great hops and pulled the appropriate lever. Silent machinery pulled the cat-o'-nine-tails tapestry out of the way, revealing the diabolical framework of the Zeta Ray!

This was the first time Roger had taken a good look at the evil machine. It was also the first time he had ever seen a small, neatly lettered sign on the front of the machine that read: PLACE JEWEL HERE.

"Bouncer's doing what da sign says!" the bunny declared. "Bouncer's turning on da machine!"

"The Zeta Ray!" Edward moaned apprehensively.

"Bouncer's swiveling da machine around so da ray will hit Mother Antoinette!" the rabbit announced.

"Oh, no, you don't!" Roger's mother replied. "Not if my whip has anything to say about it!"

Roger turned to see that Mother Antoinette once again had the whip in her hand and a sneer on her lips.

It was time for a quick Captain Crusader statement.

"The family that—"

CRACK

The close flick of the whip startled him.

"Um—" He had to regain his wits. What was he saying? Oh, yeah—"that plays together—"

CRACK *CRACK*

"Your sayings won't work on me, if I can't hear them!" Mother Antoinette laughed triumphantly. She turned her attention to Bouncer. "And as for you, you oversized rodent—"

The now-scarlet ray shot out of the Zeta machine.

"Bouncer's got da ray working!"

CRACK snapped the whip. *CRACK* *CRACK*

"The ray will never touch me!" Mother Antoinette declared.

CRACK *CRACK* *CRACK* *CRACK* *CRACK*
CRACK *CRACK* *CRACK*
CRACK *CRACK* *CRACK*
CRACK *CRACK* *CRACK*
CRACK *CRACK* *CRACK* *CRACK* *CRACK*

The whip seemed to be everywhere, snapping between Bouncer and Roger, keeping the rabbit from moving and Captain Crusader from speaking.

"Mrs. Gordon!" Delores called. "You can't keep that up forever!"

"Really?" was Mother Antoinette's amused reply. "My dear, you have never handled a whip!"

Roger realized that if the whip affected his mother the way Nut Crunchies affected him, she *might* be able to keep it up forever!

CRACK *CRACK* *CRACK* Somehow, the whip managed to land near the Plotmaster a few times, too. Actually, Roger realized, in this ruby glow the Plotmaster could be mistaken for the Great Chieftain of the Whatsahoosie.

"And don't you get any ideas, either!" Mother Antoinette called. She had gotten too good with that whip. They might be caught in a standoff—forever.

"The Zeta Ray," Edward sighed. "Who will ever miss a slime monster?"

"Brawwwwwk!" the incredibly disgusting chicken-thing declared as he launched himself at Roger's mother. The two of them rolled, together, into the ruby light.

Roger's mother stopped struggling. Both Edward and she sat up and shook their heads.

THERE!

the Plotmaster declared.

THAT'S BETTER!

And everybody started to move again. The Plotmaster snapped his fingers, and the angelic choir and backlighting were back, but, just before Roger lost sight of his face, he could have sworn he saw a strong family resemblance to Dr. Dee Dee Davenport.

"Roger?" his mother called. "What am I doing here?"

"I'll explain everything to you, Mom," Roger called back, "real soon, I promise."

"Roger!" The excitement in Delores' voice made Roger turn his head, and he saw exactly why she was excited.

She was no longer a sheep.

She grabbed Roger and kissed him; one of those long, deep, movie kisses.

Roger gasped for breath when it was over. He had to make sure his heart was still working.

"I guess we have the Plotmaster to thank!" Delores waved at the backlit man in blue.

HEY, IT'S ALL IN A DAY'S WORK.
BUT I GOTTA GO, KIDS—
I'VE GOT A CINEVERSE TO RUN!
FIRST, THOUGH, I GOTTA GET SOME OF THESE FOLKS HOME.

There was a great deal of blue smoke. Roger realized that about ninety per cent of the occupants of the room had vanished, including, to his relief, a certain foreign woman with a knife.

"Yip?" Dwight remarked.

"Dwight!" Officer O'Clanrahan called in concern. "What's the matter with you, boy?"

"Yip?" Dwight replied, not quite looking at the policeman.

"You're out of my sight for only a few hours, and this is what happens?" O'Clanrahan frowned. "Well, no more!

I've seen the error of my ways! By all that I hold dear, I renounce my life of evil!"

He patted the white German shepherd on the head.

"Yip?" Dwight repeated slowly. "Bark? Arf?" He blinked, and looked up at Officer O'Clanrahan. "Bark, yip, arf!"

The policeman grinned. "That's my Wonder Dog!"

Edward stood up. "Wait a minute! I remember now! Professor Peril exposed me to the Zeta Ray in the Institute of Very Advanced Science!"

Peril's head whipped about, searching for a means of escape. "So I was looking for more cheap help!"

Edward looked down at his slime-chicken form. "There's a zipper here somewhere." He found something right below his neck. "Ah, here it is!" With a single motion, he undid the entire front of his slime-chicken suit, and pulled it from his brown, hairy body.

"Oogie," the Prince of the Jungle called, "Zabana's favorite orangutang!"

"Zabana," the orangutang called back, "Oogie's favorite Prince of the Jungle!"

The Prince of the Jungle smiled. "Now, Zabana and Oogie go back to jungle, where we belong!"

Doc holstered both his six-guns. "Think I'll try to work back into bein' a hero."

Louie smiled and waved. "And, now that the hero's back, I get to go back to being a sidekick!"

"The bunnies get to go back to Bunnyland!" Fluffytail announced.

Doctor Dread shook his fist at the rabbits. "Malevelo can't wait until he gets back to his Mystic Kingdom. He'll get those darn bunnies yet!"

"I think I'll go into a more economical line of villainy," Professor Peril muttered as he skulked about.

Bertha shrugged her broad shoulders. "It's up to me, then, to take over the mob and get those men in line!"

"Really?" Menge cringed. "Maybe it's time for me to go back to suburbia and work on my rec room."

The Plotmaster waved to all of them.

THERE'LL ALWAYS BE A CINEVERSE—
AS LONG AS THERE'S A CAPTAIN CRUSADER TO PROTECT IT!

Then Plotmaster, chariot, and angelic choir disappeared in a cloud of blue smoke.

Roger looked at Delores. This had worked out pretty well, hadn't it?

"Roger?" his mother called. "Not to bother you, dear, but when I go home, would you mind if I held on to this whip—as a keepsake?"

THE END
OR THE BEGINNING?